GUARDIAN

OF THE

LIGHTNING

SEEDS

JOHN EUDY

ISBN 978-1-0980-9850-6 (paperback)
ISBN 978-1-0980-9851-3 (digital)

Christian Faith Publishing, Inc.
832 Park Avenue
Meadville, PA 16335
www.christianfaithpublishing.com

Printed in the United States of America

For my daughters Angela and Abigail, and my brother Jared. I hope to see you again one day.

To Saint Kateri Tekakwitha (Lily of the Mohawk) and Blessed Ukon "Justo" Takayama (Samurai of Christ). May their prayers be the bridge that brings all peoples together for Christ Jesus.

CONTENTS

PRELUDE
FRUIT OF THE TREE OF LIFE

Fire crackles and embers rise swiftly and gently to the starlit night sky. Firelight dances around casting shadows on the surrounding trees and rocks. An old chieftain and a young man sit silently on opposite sides of the fire. Though weary, the old chief sits up straight and still, his legs crossed in front of him. He stares at the fire, his once blazing brown eyes are fixated on the tips of the flame as they dance in the night sky. The jet-black hair of his youth has turned almost silver but is still clean, neatly braided and rests on each shoulder.

Many seasons have come and gone for him. He has walked many lands, seen the deep beauty of Mother Nature and fought against the darkest of evils. Etched in the wrinkles that now cover his brown-skinned face is the wisdom of his age; the experience of a good life. His old fingers lay gently upon the weathered-spirit stick across his lap. The short staff has deep and long burn marks at its base with strange markings (蛍 雷光) near its top. An enormously long and mysterious black feather with a blue tip and a white edge all along its inner vane is tied with a leather strip from the top of it. The feather is as long as the spirit stick itself.

"The embers dance like fireflies," the chief says softly and slowly. "They remind me of another time. They remind me of my brother-friends, the Hotaru-Raikō,[1] and of the quest I went on as a young warrior. The embers also remind me that my time here is at an end." His old eyes focus through the fire onto the young man sitting across from him, who listens with open mouth and gleaming eyes.

"It is your time now, Elu[2]. You have completed your rites of passage into manhood and must take up the mantle of protector when I go."

"Of the lightning seeds, Grandfather?" He says a bit eagerly.

"Yes. Those and your tribe. You have learned the sacred value of both. We are unique amongst other tribes. Our history and our charge to protect the lightning seeds makes us so. You are a man now, Elu, and if you are to be wise, you must know the full history of our tribe and how we came to protect the lightning seeds."

Chief Hania pauses for a moment. "Let me take you back to the beginning."

*****

All life comes from the Great Mysterious One. He set Father Sun and Mother Earth in the sky and blessed their union. The undying warmth of Sun entered the bosom of Mother Earth, who conceived both flora and fauna. The Great Spirit poured out all his goodness into the land, the water, and the sky. Then he created the first man. In the beginning, First Man was good and was at peace in the unspoiled lands. Though he lived in harmony with beast and

---

[1] Pronounced ho-tar-oo rheye-koh (Horaru is firefly and Raiko is lightning, translated from Japanese).
   Not an actual word combination in Japanese, this is my name for these unique characters.
[2] Name means *full of grace*.

plant, he was lonely. Little Boy Man was created, and First Man became Elder Brother.

Elder Brother was content in teaching and guiding Little Boy Man from infancy to manhood. All the animal tribes loved Little Boy Man for he was friendly and kind. He, in turn, learned their ways and language. They were all happy until the evil spirit came.

Unk-to-mee, the spider, the troublemaker, the deceiver, saw Little Boy Man grow in wisdom and ingenuity. He feared man would be the master of all animals. He convinced all the animal tribes to turn against man. Unk-to-mee brought war upon the earth, forever dividing the trail between man and animal. Elder Brother saw this treachery and gave Little Boy Man bow, arrow, war club, and spear. With these weapons he easily repelled his enemy. Soon after the defeat of Unk-to-mee, Boy Man entered a second battle, this time with the elements.

In autumn, Elder Brother and Boy Man prepared a warm tent and stored up food for the winter. So much snow fell that winter that only the tips of man's teepee poles could be seen in the deep cold snow. The fierce, and very hungry, animal tribes came to finally kill Man, but they were stopped by Father Sun who melted the snow, causing a great flood. Elder Brother and Young Man rode out the flood waters in their birch bark canoe while only a few of the animal tribes were saved from it. In the end, man had finally conquered animal and withstood the elements.

The Great Spirit was disturbed by the wars and violence though. As punishment, he denied Elder Brother, Man, and all the animal tribes' access to the *tree of life*, the fruit of which gives eternal life to those who eat of it. The *tree of life* grows from the light of the creator himself. Its trunk of light once grew in turquoise laden rocks. Its branches danced and spun in many upward directions. Its canopy was the clouds, which, like the seasons, changed colors each day with the sunrise and sunset. Fireflies with dark bodies, burgundy heads, and gray wings, danced in the lush grassy fields around it, flashing their bright golden lights in gratitude for both the life they had been given and for each other's company.

The tree bore the most amazing fruit in those days, round and lightning filled. They sparkled in the canopy. Unfortunately, it was ripe with fruit during the time when it became forbidden. The Great Spirit sent his servants to harvest the lightning seeds from it. Then he placed fierce-winged warriors around the tree so man could not return to it. The great tree remained dormant, sleeping until the price for man and animal's transgressions were paid for.

Many seasons passed. Peace returned between the descendants of Boy Man and the land they wandered. Knowledge of the tree and its location was lost to them. However, the creator who still loves his children, sought a relationship with Man again. He looked down upon his creation and saw our ancestors. He was truly pleased with how well they lived in harmony with the world. Because they were honorable, peaceful, and just, he entrusted the lightning seeds to our clan as a sign of trust. The winged warrior who brought them instructed our ancestors to keep them safe and hidden. Planting them was forbidden. The creator said he would come back for the seeds one day. That he would sow them, and at the appropriate time, would harvest a bounty of fruit to be given to his faithful children so they might live forever.

Now, before even First Man, there was another mighty winged warrior, a servant in the Great Mysterious One's presence. His name was Lucifer, which meant *light bearer*. He witnessed all the creator made but took no pleasure in it. Envy and resentment blackened his heart. He wanted the creator's power and title—to rule over Father Sun, Mother

Earth, and all of creation. Lucifer rebelled but could not defeat the creator. He was cast down, plummeting from the sky to the underworld like a bolt of lightning. He lost all his light as he fell, becoming the bearer of darkness instead. He was forever exiled from the spirit lands.

Brooding in his emptiness, the evil spirit contemplated ways to corrupt Man and the lands he inhabited. He used Unk-to-mee to sow mistrust among the animal tribes and start the first wars. After the flood, and over the ages, he sent disease upon the land and into the animals. He poisoned waters and the fish that swam in them. He corrupted the spirits of weak men—teaching them evil magic and instilling in them selfishness, jealousy, and hatred of their brothers and sisters. Then in time, he learned about the gift of the lightning seeds to our ancestors. From then on, his desire to steal them was insatiable. The evil spirit wanted to grow his own perverse grove rooted in the rotten soil of his hell, twisting and corrupting their fruit. The fruit from his *trees of ruin* would bring death, destruction, and damnation to all who ate of it.

The evil spirit searched for many moons before learning the lightning seeds were hidden deep in the heart of our dwellings at Mesa Verde.

1

THIEF IN THE NIGHT

Many generations of warriors guarded the seeds, keeping them safe and hidden. We knew who each warrior was because they were always given names of a powerful element like *Sacred Wind* or *Rain Bringer*. Their dress was always adorned with some elemental symbolism too. Over time however, their number dwindled, and our defense of the seeds became complacent; relaxed. By my time, Chief Ouray,[3] my father, felt the lightning seeds were hidden well enough and that our tribe had greater worries than the creator's seeds.

As is tradition, my mother gave me over to my father and uncles at the age of eight to begin my warrior's training. My grandfather passed on the knowledge of the seeds to me at the age of ten. He also taught me history, traditions, and a little humor. My uncle taught me how to navigate the land, to hunt, and to fight. My father taught me how to understand the moods of Mother Nature, how to forage from her bounty, and how to trade with other clans and tribes. He also instructed me on diplomacy—how to keep peace and prepare for war. I listened to their instruction with reverent silence as I readied myself to enter manhood.

---

[3] Pronounced oh-rey. The name means *the arrow* (Also the name of a great *Ute* Chief circa mid to late 1800s).

During my fifteenth year, while I was preparing for the *eneepee* or vapor bath and the other rites of passage, the evil spirit was busy sending his minor servants who came in many forms to test our reactions and our resolve. Finding our defense of the seeds was lax, he sent his servant Lost One, a cunning skinwalker, to steal them from us. Lost One came in the form of brother coyote, the trickster, on a night with no moon in the sky. He slipped quietly into our dwellings and past tribesmen as they slept. His acute sense of smell sniffing out his prize. He found the sacred room and opened the creaking door just enough to slip past. There in the darkness, the seed's white subtle glow emanated from the most ornate bowl-shaped basket our ancestors had ever weaved.

The Lost One approached the basket. He removed the leather bags he had carried over his back with his mouth and sat them next to the table upon which the basket sat. He stood on his hind legs clumsily reaching for and grasping the basket with his front paws. He awkwardly poured the contents out into the bags and then tossed the basket into the corner. He did not notice the single seed miss his bag and land in the sand. He covered the flaps of the bags, and then, using his long nose, parted the bags and slipped through the arch so they rested on his back. When he turned to leave, his paw twisted more sand on top of the dropped seed, hiding it.

He nudged the door open a little more to widen the gap enough for his now full packs to fit through. As Lost One cautiously slipped past the door, a young brave, woken from the scuffling sounds, noticed the coyote coming out of the forbidden room. He raised his torch so he could get a better look and not only noticed the packs on the large coyote's back, but also his odd eyes. They did not glow the same color as a normal coyote. They looked like a man's eyes. The courageous young warrior knew something was wrong. Though he feared the skinwalker, his courage was stronger. He drew his knife from its sheath on his belt and ran toward the coyote. Lost One quickly rushed out, angered by his discovery. The brave gave chase, yelling a loud war cry to wake the tribe. Unfortunately, it was not long before he lost sight of the wily coyote in the darkness.

Several tribesmen searched the grounds for the coyote but to no avail. He had already made his escape in the dark moonless night. It was near daybreak when Chief Ouray went to inspect the forbidden room where the seeds were kept. He opened the door and stood with sadness at the room's desecration. He knew he had failed the creator but didn't know what to do next. He bent down to pick up the basket when a glint of light caught his eye. He scooped up the sand with the remaining seed in it. Blowing the dust from his hand, he stared down at the luminous seed glowing in his hand. It had been years since he had taken the time to look closely at one. It was the shape of a maize kernel but with a thin translucent outer skin. Tiny arcs of lightning flashed within its soft white glow, making it appear to flicker. It was more beautiful than any precious stone.

In a moment of fear and doubt, he decided to plant the last seed. He thought if he were able to grow a new tree to fruition, he could replace the lost seeds and therefore, avoid any calamity brought down on his people. Many generations had passed since the creator's emissary had visited the tribe, so my father, in his momentary weakness, did not think the growth and harvesting of a single small tree would be noticed.

Chief Ouray called for the tribal healer, Wounded Crow, and the elders to don their ceremonial dress and gather at the foot of Mesa Verde to conduct a rain dance in the early morning hours. I was not invited to participate in the dance; however, since I had begun the rites of passage into manhood, my father instructed me to come close and watch. The elders, and other respected tribesmen, gathered around a small open patch of land. I sat near a sage bush on a little hill near the site. It was close enough and high enough that I would be able to see the ceremony.

The Chief and the healer stood on opposite sides of the patch of land. My father approached the center with the glowing seed in hand. He gently planted it there before moving back near the edge of the outcropping. The drumbeat started slowly. The two men stepped toward each other, back, then turned and began to dance slowly around the seed. Rhythmic chanting accompanied the circular dance. Wounded Crow's dance purified the land, while my father called for the life-giving rains.

The patch of ground appeared to take on a lighter tan color while rain clouds moved slowly over the cliffs. The tribe continued their rhythmic drumming, chanting, and dancing until the first drops of cool rain began to fall. The ground turned darker as it became saturated. Then, sizzling, sparkling, and crackling, a small piece of light broke through the surface of the ground. The tribe continued its ritual. The crooked light shot up into the sky like lightning.

Unlike normal lightning though, it did not give way to the thunder that follows; it stayed connected to the ground. A small white fire burned around the base of its trunk. The bolt grew outward. The blazing tree formed branches of static white light. Storm clouds caught in its offshoots formed the tree's canopy. Wounded Crow, spirit stick in hand, and my father, Chief Ouray, continued to dance around the edges of the flashing trunk. Arcs of the purest white light randomly connected with the healer's staff, leaving burnt streaks in one end. It was working, the seed produced an enormous tree.

Suddenly, the tree imploded with an unexpected, mighty thunderclap. An outflowing ring of sound which not only reverberated in my chest but knocked everyone to the ground. Elders, tribesmen, Wounded Crow, and my father had all been thrown several feet away from the patch of land. Even a few pine and juniper trees close by had been knocked down by the wave of sound. I wiped the settling dust from my eyes. The sky was clearing and the lightning tree was gone. In its place, at the center of the patch of now glass-like ground, stood a mighty winged warrior.

He was easily three heads taller than our tallest warrior. He was of a race I did not know. He stood with his arms crossed and his enormous brilliant white wings stretched out at an upward angle to his right and left. He wore a deep blue armor (the kind of which I had never seen), over a light gray shirt. His armor and belt were made of gold. A long sheath with some sort of elongated knife hung from his side. I knew this must be the legendary "Wind Walker," who visited my ancestors. He unfolded his arms, tucked his wings to his back and walked swiftly toward my father, who, raising himself up out of the dirt, knelt on the ground in reverence. It was the only time I had ever seen my father kneel.

The angel stood over him for a moment, before sternly saying, "Do you know what you have done, Ouray? Did you think it was you who brought the rain? No! It is the Great Spirit who sends the rain when you dance. Did you think he would not notice why you asked for the rain; what you were doing? Were you not told planting the lightning seeds was forbidden? Seeds from the *tree of life* were yours to protect; they are neither yours to plant, nor yours to reap from. You have disobeyed the Great Spirit."

My father had no words. He simply turned his head downward in regretful silence. Wind Walker took a deep breath, leaned down, and lifted him up from the dirt. His tone softened, "My friend, you have lost all of the lightning seeds," he said with great sadness. "You were not vigilant; you let a thief take them from your home. The Creator is disappointed and justifiably angered," he paused.

Chief Ouray humbly lifted his head. "I know now I have done a great wrong, Wind Walker. I have broken my tribe's ancestral treaty and will accept my fate. All I ask is that he does not curse my people."

Wind Walker sighed. "He is merciful. You shall not die, nor shall your people be cursed." He paused in uncomfortable silence. "However, because you have shown such open disregard for the trust he put in your people, you must make amends. Here, in Mesa Verde, your people have become unbalanced. So your people with leave this place and never return. It is time for your people to travel with the seasons once more. You must trust in the land that your people will be provided what they need to live. You will soon be blessed with a vision of a land north of here. You will lead them there. Furthermore, you must send your only son—" without even looking in my direction, Wind Walker lifted his mighty arm and pointed to where I partially hid among the sage, "Notah[4], to recover the seeds without delay."

I sat down upon the ground in shock. I looked at my father, who turned his head toward me, and then down for a moment. We both knew he could not argue or sway Wind Walker if he were to keep the tribe safe. This task would not only be just punishment for my father's misdeed but would become my rite of passage into manhood. Though I did not show it, deep down I was afraid. There was much uncertainty and great unknown in this task.

My father looked back up at the angel. "It will be done as you say."

---

[4] Pronounced no-tah, the name means "almost there."

"Chief Ouray," Wind Walker reassured, "I know you have been preparing Notah to become a man. You have taught him properly. He knows the kinship your people share with the land and the animal tribes. You have taught him how to fish, to hunt, to forage, and to clothe himself. You have taught him how to fight and to survive. You have taught him to see the sacred spirit in all things. Still, I see concern in your eyes." Wind Walker made a long pause. "He will not go alone. I will call the Hotaru-Raikō to accompany him." My father looked inquisitively at the angel.

Wind Walker turned toward me. He motioned to me with his hand. "Come here, Notah." I stood up and approached with a fearful respect. I felt like a small boy standing next to giants. Wind Walker turned and leaned toward me. Placing his mighty hand on my shoulder, he said in a low tone, "You have little time, Lost One is swiftly moving west. Retrieve your bow, a full quiver, your knife, netting, and blanket. Fill a pack with two water skins and two days provisions. Return here as soon as you are finished. Go."

I turned and ran as fast as I could to my dwelling in Mesa Verde. My mind racing as fast as my legs carried me. I did not question the instructions given, rather I obeyed willingly because I knew this task was for my tribe, not just for me. Nor did I think to pause and take a last look at that place, even though I knew it would be the last time I saw it.

"Chief Ouray, tell your elders to prepare your tribe for the journey," instructed Wind Walker. "They are to take only what they need to survive, no unnecessary possessions. You will leave on the second sunrise from today." My father turned and walked calmly to where his elders had gathered. They were close enough to have overheard Wind Walker, but he gave them more detailed instructions and assigned specific tasks. They nodded in agreement and returned to the rest of the tribe.

Only the healer and my father had remained with Wind Walker until I returned. They stood in silence, listening to Wind Walker. "If Notah is successful, your tribe will return to its migratory life, moving with the seasons and flowing with the land again. You will be blessed with descendants who will create new beautiful baskets to keep the seeds safe and hidden in." I did not realize how much of the day had passed but Father Sun was already past his highest peak when I came back.

"Good," said Wind Walker as I approached. "I will call the Hotaru-Raikō now." He turned to face west. The sun still shown bright in the clear blue western sky. He raised his left hand and said in a loud, but low octave, "*Detekuru*[5]!" His voice echoed down the canyon. He then turned back toward me, leaned down slightly, and gave me instructions for the journey.

"Notah, you are to journey to the place called *Tomesha*[6]. You know of this place, yes?"

"Yes," I answered.

"There is an old dead tree still standing in the desolate basin there. You will know it as soon as you see its petrified remains. At its base is an entrance to the ancient underground city called *Shin-au-av*[7]. The one you know as Lost One stole the lightning seeds and travels now to hide them there. You must enter the cavernous city, which has been claimed by wickedness, find and retrieve the seeds. I have called the Hotaru-Raikō to aid you in your journey."

He paused for a moment. "Along the way, I want you to weave a basket out of sweet agave fibers to carry the seeds in. You may include other plants, but the basket must be some-

---

[5] Pronounced day-tay-kir-oo—"come forth" (translated from Japanese).
[6] *Ground afire*, roughly translated from *Shoshone* aka Death Valley.
[7] *God's land* or *Ghost land*, roughly translated from *Paiute*.

thing worthy to hold such a prize; something you can carry on your back too."

Wind Walker looked up and pointed at the sky. In a very somber voice he said, "The evil spirit plans to lay claim to the seeds when the next full moon rides high in the sky. You, son of Ouray, must accomplish this task before it rises. Do you understand?"

"Yes," I said.

"Use the tracking skills you were taught to pursue him there." Continued Wind Walker. "He is following the north side of the Old Age River[8]. You too should stay on the north side to avoid enemy tribes to the south. You will have to swim across Aha Kwahwat[9] where it meets the Old Age River. You should be able to pick his tracks back up on the north side of Aha Kwahwat. Stay out of the Great Canyon. When Aha Kwahwat turns south, you will continue due west thru Red Rock Canyon, and across the eastern side of the Mojave to the Black Mountains. There you can enter Tomesha thru the Old Queen's Pass[10]."

A low humming sound slowly grew from the western canyons. Out of the corner of my eye, I saw Wounded Crow search the horizon, but Wind Walker paid him and the sound no attention. Instead, he stood upright again and still looking deep into my eyes said, "Remember what your clan has taught you, Notah. Travel wisely. Keep sight of Brother Eagle in the sky. Not only will he help guide you west but he will also serve as a messenger between you and the Great Spirit. If you need help, ask. The creator will send it." He smiled at me, and then turned his eyes westward.

We waited listening to the increasing sound of buzzing. Father Sun sank lower in the crisp spring sky, turning a

---

[8] A.k.a. San Juan River
[9] A.k.a. Colorado River
[10] A.k.a. Dante's View

dark orange as it settled between the mountains to the west. Coming down out of the dusky sky were many small white lights. At first they looked like a swarm of small stars swerving and flickering as they moved down into the river valley. They travelled up the ancient riverbed swirling about like fireflies until they got close to us. Though they moved like them, I could see they were not fireflies. Catching a short glimpse of them as they hummed by, the Hotaru-Raikō appeared human but flew on insect wings. They rose back up into the pink and purple sky before landing along the cliff edge over Mesa Verde.

Wind Walker moved to a nearby cottonwood tree. One of them broke away from the swarm and came down to speak with him. Although they only appeared roughly 8 to 10 inches tall, the Hotaru-Raikō was clearly some sort of warrior class. Their leader dressed in armor I had never seen before. Every part of his body was covered except for his eyes and hands. Upon landing, he tucked long insect-like wings behind his back while untying a long and decorative dark red rope holding his metal helmet and face mask on, both of which were also dark red in color. He removed them, exposing his pale-colored face, placed them at his side and bowed low to the angel.

When he stood, I noticed much of his chest, shoulder, waist, and leg armor was made of overlapping medal pieces like scales on a snake. Almost all of it was black. Parts of his leg armor glinted white in the twilight almost like a firefly. He wore a sleeveless thigh length overcoat over his armor which was a very dark gray trimmed in white. Running horizontal through his dark gray belt were two elongated knives. He had all the coloring of an actual firefly but was human in appearance.

The warrior spoke with the angel in a language I did not understand. Wind Walker turned to look at me, the warrior kept his attention on the angel. "Notah, come here." I immediately walked to his side. He motioned with his right hand toward the strange warrior. "This is Takeda Kenshin. He is their *Daimyō*[11]; their leader. You must show him much respect." I nodded in silence.

He returned the introduction, "Takeda-san, this Notah. Son of Chief Ouray. His name means "almost there."

Takeda quickly inspected me, then let out a half grunt, half laugh. "*Hrmph*. We will bring him the rest of the way, *masutā*.[12]" His words caught me off guard. Instead of being somewhat insulted by his tone, I was in awe that I actually understood what he said.

Wind Walker looked down at me and, probably because of the stunned look on my face, let out a short laugh. No one had ever heard him laugh before. "Ha, ha. I know you will, my friend. I know you will. Go, prepare your samurai and *ashigaru*[13]." He then turned to me, smiled and said, "From now on, you will understand his language, and he yours. It must be so you can accomplish this task. Takeda Kenshin is a seasoned warrior and good leader. Learn from him, as you have learned from your tribesmen. They may not be as big as you, but you can trust him with your life, he will defend you."

He placed his hand on my shoulder, slightly adjusting the leather strap of my quiver. "You will learn about each other on your journey. Your people and theirs share many traits and customs. The Hotaru-Raikō are uniquely suited to this journey as they too are used to living between wilderness and water. If you rely on each other, you will succeed, Notah. Also, when the time comes, the creator will send his spirit to

---

[11] Pronounced die-eem-yo—"feudal lord" (translated from Japanese).
[12] Pronounced mas-oo-tah—"master" (translated from Japanese).
[13] Pronounced ah-shee-gah-ru—"Japanese foot soldiers."

you so you may be strong of heart. Now, say farewell to your father, it is time to leave."

I went to my father, Chief Ouray. I did my best to show no fear. He placed his hands upon my shoulders, looked deep in my eyes, and said, "I know you will make amends for our tribe, my son. I have faith in you. When I see you again, you will be a man." He patted me, and then released me.

I turned to leave but Wounded Crow, who had been silent the whole time called my name. I turned back to see him holding out his spirit stick—the one he used during the rain dance. "Notah, take this with you. It will protect you."

He approached and slowly placed the short staff into my quiver. I turned back to face him. "You have been preparing for manhood and your vision quest." He paused. "There will be no vision quest for you. This journey will fulfill all the tasks to initiate the dream. I suspect that when you return to us, you will have found your purpose and the answers to many questions. We will offer a pipe in gratitude when you return. Go now." He turned and walked back to my father's side. I looked one more time at my father, who smiled at me, then held up his hand in farewell.

All the Hotaru-Raikō had already left the cliff top and were flying west toward the setting sun. Only three stayed back, the *Daimyō*, Takeda Kenshin, and two others. They hovered a short distance in front of me. Takeda tied his helmet and his fierce mask back on, took his spear from one of the other warriors; and then motioned to follow them, saying, "*Yukō*,[14] Notah-kun."

---

[14] Pronounced yee-koh—"let's go" (translated from Japanese).

2

JOURNEY WITH THE HOTARU-RAIKŌ

旅

Notah is a normal wiry youth, full of energy. His hair is braided, and a simple cloth headband keeps his hair back and the sweat out of his eyes. He dressed light and had little to carry, which allows for a swift journey. He wears sturdy leather moccasins, leather leggings, a cloth breechcloth tucked over his belt, and a lightweight buckskin shirt. His blanket lay over his right shoulder, and is fastened with a second belt holding his knife, waterskins, and small pouch of food. His simple leather quiver and bow case also straddle his right shoulder.

That first night, after departing Mesa Verde, Notah follows the canyon as far south as he can in the dark before finding a safe place for them all to rest. Still adjusting to each other's company, the group travels in relative silence the next day. A young brave is normally expected to go out into nature alone as part of his rite of passage into manhood. This journey is different though. Notah watches the Hotaru-Raikō carefully. His new companions are unlike anything he has ever seen in nature before. They too watch Notah trying to learn from his habits, tracking skills, and more. The silence that pervades the party is not due to mistrust, rather it is a sense of unfamiliarity that drives their quiet observation of each other. Deep down, they all know that trust is something to be earned over time.

Notah knew the land north of Old Age River well. He follows the wash south to Wounded Hand River[15], which flows directly west into Old Age River. There, he can move quickly along the valley floor and out into open flat lands where he can run at a slow steady pace. He makes stops when necessary, but with the ability to fly, the Hotaru-Raikō easily stay close to him.

This journey was quite different than others he has made with his father and uncle. Those trips had a simpler meaning, often hunting or trading expeditions with other tribes. They traveled slower then. He was taught to harmonize with Mother Nature, to understand her movements, on each of those trips. His father and uncle constantly asked him questions about natural events, to see if he could identify plants, animal tracks, sources of water, weather patterns, and so on. While he was confident in his survival skills, it was the coming conflict to regain the lightning seeds that gnawed at the back of his mind.

*****

By the evening of the second day, the group exits the valley and enters the flat land west of Mesa Verde. They set up a small camp there, just before sunset. Notah takes the time to point out edible plants to Takeda and his samurai, ensuring they can eat along the way. There is only a tiny sliver of a moon in the sky that night, most of the light coming from a small campfire. Notah is quietly nibbling on the pine

---

[15] A.k.a. Mancos River

nuts from his pouch and observing the starry trail in the night sky. He wonders if it leads to the great beyond, to the spirit lands. Sasaki Nakamura comes to sit on a tall stone by him. He says, "We notice you say very little, Notah-kun."

"I was taught it was better to listen and to watch if one wants to learn," replies Notah politely.

"Very good," he replies, "I am Sasaki Nakamura. I am samurai." He gives a slight bow. "Thank you for showing us the cactus flower."

"You're welcome, Nakamura-san." Notah pauses. "Did I address you correctly?"

"Yes," Says, Sasaki with a smile. The two have a short conversation, which is watched by all, and each grows decidedly more comfortable with one another that very evening.

*****

The next day, Notah washes himself in the river just before daybreak. He then stands erect with hands raised to shoulder height, offering his thanks to Father Sun, who rises over his old home in the east. The bright rays warm his body and help him dry. He collects his gear, makes sure the fire is fully extinguished and scattered into the earth, and then departs slowly at first. Although he could follow Wounded Hand River all the way to Old Age River, Notah decides to turn northwest and quicken his pace across the flat ground to save time. They reach what Notah believes is the Old Age River valley as the sun starts to set that very day.

The next morning, they wake to cool, spring air. A chilly dewfall has blanketed their camp, letting them know they are indeed close to the river. Remembering Lost One would be travelling this way, Notah begins to watch for mixed animal and human tracks as they travel west. If he can find cougar or coyote tracks interchanging with human tracks, then he knows he is on Lost One's trail.

Notah explains to the *Daimyō*, as well as his samurai Sasaki Nakamura and Hatano Yoshimoto, how to look for the tracks and what they looked like. Sasaki and Hatano then pass the details on to their *ashigaru*. It isn't long before one of them find human tracks leading up to one side of a small stream, a tributary to the Old Age River, and coyote tracks departing the exact opposite side of it. *Lost One must have stopped to drink, rest, and then change into coyote to pick up speed.* Thinks Notah. The *ashigaru* split into two bands, each one led by one of the samurai. Now that they know what to look for, they alternate days searching and tracking Lost One's prints, which helps Notah travel confidently. Working together to track the enemy builds further trust and confidence among them.

*****

Old Age River turns south slightly before coming back north into a large bend. There is high flat ground there, between an offshoot of the Aha Kwahwat and Old Age River. After the bend, the river turns south again before flowing west and running into Aha Kwahwat. Notah decides to leave the river valley and travel southwest in a straight line on that higher ground. Since the river might be a little higher from spring flooding, it will be easier to cross well north of the confluence at a narrower bend.

He soon finds a suitable spot between a northern tributary and the confluence. The water is swift but not too deep. If it were summer, this part of the river would be a simple deep-water fording. Notah points out a narrow crack in the canyon rim on the western side of the river leading back up to higher ground[16]. "That is where we can reach the high flat ground again," he says. Takeda agrees to lead the *ashigaru* to scout the path up the canyon. Sasaki and Hatano volunteer to stay with Notah as he crosses the fast waters. They, along with two other soldiers, also offer to carry Notah's bow, full quiver, blanket, and clothes over the river, keeping them all dry. He is grateful for their kindness too. He strips down to his breechcloth and moccasins. Those that stayed behind collect his gear and head across the river behind Takeda's scouting party.

Notah heads upstream a little. He knows the water will carry him downriver as he crosses. He stops on the bank and casts a stick upstream and observes how fast the rushing water carries it past. As he wades in, he finds the water cool and refreshing. The deeper he goes, the more he can feel it push against his legs. He knows he will be swept off his feet once he is chest-deep. He pauses waist-deep in the water for a moment. He looks up to see Sasaki and Hatano hovering in the air just out ahead of him; they nod to give him confidence. He looks downstream one more time to see his goal before plunging in the river and starting to swim.

The water instantly carries him away like the stick. He swims slightly into the current as strongly as he can, but it feels like he is going downstream faster than he is crossing. He fights against the swift water. Determined to make it across, he concentrates on his strokes and taking a breath when he can. He puts all his strength into it.

Although it has only been two or three minutes, to Notah, it feels like he has been struggling in the water for a long time. He is running out of energy quickly. His arms and legs smack the water like brother beaver's tail when he gives a warning to strangers. Before long, the samurai call out to him, letting him know he is near the bank. He quickly lifts

[16] See Hole-in-the-Rock, Utah

his head to see, drops his foot, and feels the ground below. It is still too deep to walk though so he makes a final push, half swimming and bouncing on the riverbed. He is finally able to stand in the river. He is breathing heavily; his arms and legs are week and he can barely stand against the rushing water.

Notah walks slowly up to the bank, stopping thigh deep in the river. With his hands at his waist and water dripping from his soaked hair and body, he bends over to catch his breath. He stands back upright and looks around. He has gone a short distance past his goal, but not too far. He continues up onto the dry riverbank, turns, and flops down upon his rear in the loose gravel. He is exhausted. The samurai land close by Sasaki says, "You did well, Notah-kun."

Notah, still breathing hard, nods in gratitude. "Now you know what it is like for us to fly into a strong wind." And the two samurai give a chuckle. "*Iku,*[17] the clan waits for us at the top of the pass." They take wing, and Notah slowly rises to his feet and follows them up the bank toward the gap in the canyon wall.

*****

Notah, clearly exhausted after crossing the river, decides to make camp early. He collects his blanket, bow, quiver, and clothes from the *ashigaru*. He thanks them again for carrying it all safely to the top of the canyon wall. Finding a small pinyon pine tree, he removes his wet moccasins and breechcloth, and hangs them over its branches. He places his dry blanket over his shoulder and wraps his knife belt around his waist using the blanket to cover himself while his clothes dry.

He takes a few moments to observe his surroundings. *This will be good hunting grounds for rabbit and for foraging,*

---

[17] Pronounced ee-kooh—"go" (translated from Japanese).

he thinks to himself. It has been five days since he left Mesa Verde and he is one third of the way there, so he decides to rest for a full day and restock his provisions. Fond memories of tribal rabbit drives come to mind; times when his people would congregate, socialize, dance, play games, and tell stories. He wants to share this joyous part of his culture with his newfound friends. He lets Takeda know his plans to rest and to hunt.

A while later, after his clothes have dried and he is comfortably dressed, Notah goes down into a small ravine to string his nets between two small shrubs. He gathers the Hotaru-Raikō and explains how their ability to fly and their speed will help chase rabbits into those nets. "We must be quick and wily like brother hare," he says as he draws the image of their tracks into the sand.

Notah teaches them how to find the tracks before sending them out on scouting parties. While they hunt, the *Daimyō* and two samurai help Notah forage for wild spinach, cactus blossoms, and other edibles to share.

The *ashigaru* find and enthusiastically funnel three rabbits toward the netting; Notah joins in the chase. Just as the wild hare enter the nets, one of the squad leaders, whose name was Hasegawa, gets distracted. He flies into the side of a branch and tumbles down into the net. Not noticing him, the rest of the soldiers quickly pull the corners of the net together. Notah jumps on the netting, gathers up the loose ends and cinches them tightly. Hasegawa is now amongst the captured hare bundled on the ground. Notah, still holding the netting down, see him and yells, "What are you doing! Get out of there! I cannot kill them until you're out of the way!"

In the confusion, Hasegawa grabs onto one their ears, which the hare immediately flops downward. He cannot hold on to the soft fur and begins to slide. The rabbit stomps at him with his hindfoot, knocking him off. Now loose in the netting, Hasegawa is pummeled by the frantic rabbits. He tries desperately to fight back, while avoiding their sharp teeth, but his kicks and punches have no effect. The net tumbles, twists, and turns, while fur flies out of it.

Hasegawa is kicked hard in the stomach and decides to give up the fight. Escape is preferable at this point. He is sandwiched between two of the rabbit's sides. He reaches up and grasps the netting. Two *ashigaru* fly to the top of the net and reach for him. They grasp his arms and pull him partway through the netting but the pole holding the banner on his back gets caught, preventing them from pulling him out. The hare kick and jostle the netting. Hasegawa lets go of his friends. Now pinned sideways against the net, he scoots his lower body around and pushes his feet through an opening. His friends move down to grab hold of his feet and yank him awkwardly through. They all land in the dusty sand; their uniforms completely disheveled and covered in rabbit fur.

Notah quickly clubs the rabbits, killing them. A little short of breath, he stands and looks down at Hasegawa and his two friends wiping sand and fur from themselves. Takeda, Hatano, Sasaki, and the other warriors, who had watched everything unfold from the branches around the netting, laugh wholeheartedly at the trio. Notah, taking a second to think about what just happened, lets out a chuckle too. He sets his club down, offers his hand to them, and says, "Ah, you did well for your first hunt, little brothers."

Hasegawa, looking up in humble uncertainty, accepts the gesture. He collects himself while in the palm of Notah's hand on the way back to the camp.

Later, at the little river feast, as it came to be known, Notah gives solemn thanks to brother rabbit's sacrifice; that they might all be nourished. He then prepares a meal for his new brother-friends, the Hotaru-Raikō. After the meal,

Takeda, Hasegawa, and a few others eat nectar from the flow-ering cacti, while Sasaki and Hatano spar with others using wooden sticks. Those sitting around the fire tease Hasegawa, who openly laughs about being caught with the rabbits and fighting with them. Notah laughs too and says, "It is custom-ary to receive a new name when a warrior achieves a great feat. To me, Hasegawa will always be known as 'Wrestles with Hare.'" Notah smiles fondly at Hasegawa.

"*Gōi sa reta*,[18]" confirms the *daimyō* in a deep voice.

Hasegawa humbly answers, "*Hai*.[19]" They both begin to laugh.

Notah and the rest of the soldiers gathered around the fire join in. Word of his new name spreads quickly among the rest that evening. They all held that night in high regard, recounting and laughing about the event throughout the rest of the journey.

Notah's laughter subsides as he looks up. He observes the simple but elegant waxing crescent moon low in the dark starlit sky. He has made good time so far. However, the dis-tance is great, and there is much to be done still.

*****

It was early morning, on the sixth day of the trek. They again wake to a cool spring air. A wet chilly dewfall has extin-guished the fire. The cool morning air is invigorating. Notah rekindles the fire from still warm coals buried under the ash. Takeda, Hatano, Sasaki, and a few of the others gather around to warm themselves for the coming day's journey. Notah has taught his brother-friends something of his heritage but real-izes he still has much to learn from them. So with much eagerness, he asks, "*Daimyō*, I have so many questions. Will

---

18 Pronounced go-ee-sah-reh-tah—"agreed." (translated from Japanese).
19 Pronounced hi-ee—"yes." (translated from Japanese).

you teach me about your tribe? Where did you come from? How did you come into service of the Great Spirit?"

"Hmph," grunts Takeda warming his hands by the small fire. "So many questions, Notah-kun. However, if you agree to let me ride on your shoulder, I will be your *sensei*[20] for today's journey."

Notah readily agrees, gathers his things, and brakes camp. They head southwest on the high ground overlooking the river. The *daimyō* lights upon the blanket over Notah's right shoulder. He takes a seat, with his legs hanging in front of Notah's shoulder and supports himself by holding onto the bow sticking up from his bow case and quiver. It proves to be a comfortable place to be as they travel.

Takeda tells him the history of his people:

"We were there at the beginning when the first man was sent out of the garden into the earth. My clan once danced in the lush grassy fields around the great white *tree of life*. We brewed the most delicious tea from the leaves that fell from it, which is what gives us our long lives. We often celebrated our existence, our lands, and our love for Kami[21], the one you know as the Great Spirit, with elaborate tea ceremonies too. Unfortunately, it was our pride and our quest for the perfect cup of tea that led to our downfall. In our pride, we decided to make a shimmering white tea from new leaves on the *tree of life*.

"What we did not understand was that it was Kami who made the leaves fall for us. We had no right to pluck them from the tree. We dishonored Him by taking what was his and not respecting the gift he was already giving us. He was offended, and we were disgraced. Like your father, he showed us mercy. Instead of casting us down as he did the evil spirit, he only sent us out of the garden to serve our smaller cous-

---

[20] Pronounced sen-say-i—"teacher" (translated from Japanese).

[21] Pronounced kahm-ee—"God" (translated from Japanese).

ins. My clan was sent to what is now known as the Echizen Province in a land called Nihon[22]. We pledged our lives in service to our Hotaru cousins to make up for our poor judgment. We became warriors and guardians in the court of a great Hotaru lord. Our cousins do not have human forms like us, but still have many of the same customs.

"We lived and served on the south, and more sunny side, of the Fukui castle moats. The water is shallow, and the lotus lilies grow large and luxuriant. The Lord of the fireflies, whose name is Hi-ō, lives deep in the heart of one of the great pink flowers. He has only one daughter, the lovely princess Hotaru-himé. It is she who gave us the name Hotaru-Raikō because the light of our armor and weapons is white like lightning instead of the soft, golden glow they possess. While still a child, the princess was kept safely at home within the pink petals of the lily, never even going to the edges except to see her father fly off on his journeys. At least one of my samurai and two of my warriors always accompanied him to keep him safe.

"Every night the fire glowed in Hotaru-himé's body. Her light growing brighter and brighter, until it was as last as mellow as gold, illuminating the lotus like a paper lantern in a globe of coral. She waited dutifully until she was of age, then her father said, 'My daughter is now of ready, she may fly abroad with me, and when the proper suitor comes, she may marry whom she will.'

"So Hotaru-himé flew with her father in the twilight sky among the lotus lilies of the moat, then into rich rice fields, and at last far-off to the western meadows. We proudly escorted them whenever she went for a crowd of suitors always followed. She had the singular power of attracting all the night-flying insects to herself; however, she cared not for

---

[22] Pronounced nee-hohn—"Japan" (translated from Japanese).

their attention. Although she spoke politely to them all, she gave encouragement to none.

"Upon her return, Hotaru-himé was arrayed in her most resplendent robes and set on the throne in the heart of the majestic lotus. There she awaited her suitors. The queen gave us orders to keep them all at a respectful distance lest some foolish brute, dazzled by her light, should approach too near and hurt the princess or shake her throne.

"Suitor after suitor appeared, each in his own way, to woo the daughter of the King. Some were proud, some were humble, some were bold, others meek. Some flattered, or boasted, while others came with tears. Some sang to Hotaru-himé. Each one offered his love, but regardless of their wooing, each one received the same, simple answer, 'Bring me fire, and I will be your bride.'

"Each suitor, thinking he alone knew how to retrieve the fire she sought, sped away without telling his rivals. But none ever returned with fire, nor won the princess' hand in marriage. Poor suitors! The lucky few only lost their antennae, scorched their shining bodies, or singed their powdered wings. Most perished in flame or oil. Their bodies lay black and cold the next morning, dead from their foolish quests.

"Now, a young prince, who had recently ascended to the throne after his father's passing, ruled the north side of the castle moat and the fields beyond. His name was Hi-maró. He received word of the princess, her many suitors, and her request for fire. A noble and proper young firefly, prince Hi-maró sent his emissary to king Hi-ō, formally requesting permission to court his daughter. The king was pleased with the prince's courtesy and approved his courtship, with the single caveat that he too must fulfill his daughter's request for fire.

"Out of respect for both Hi-ō and Hi-maró, I sent my two best samurai, Nakamura-san and Yoshimoto-san, whom you have met, and four of my bravest *ashigaru* to escort the Prince. They kept him and his glittering battalion safe from the frogs and toads in the moat. The night of his arrival saw the lotus palace aglow with the golden light of his army, yet their glorious blaze still paled next to the regal splendor of Hotaru-himé.

"Undaunted, Hi-marō entered the court of Hi-ō. He opened his shell filling the room with red, orange, and yellow lights, which danced on the walls of the lotus like the light of a fire. Driven by the passion in his heart for the lovely princess, the prince possessed a light unlike any other Hotaru. The changing colors of his abdomen, like that of a flame, instantly attracted the eye of the princess. He approached her and humbly offered his hand for the dance. She eagerly, but politely, placed her hand in his, and then looked to her father for approval."

Takeda pauses for a moment. "I was standing behind the throne that night overseeing the court. I saw what the king saw, Prince Hi-marō brought the princess the unquenchable fire of true love. There was a deep happiness in her eyes and a glow upon her supple face. Hi-ō nodded his approval with much satisfaction. The prince wooed the princess that very night and, before he departed for his own kingdom, she agreed to marry him. They were married by the light of the next full moon and their two kingdoms became one. A great peace came over the tiny kingdom.

Soon after, Kami called for us. It is his desire for us to complete this great quest with you. By helping you retrieve the lightning seeds, we too may redeem ourselves in his sight."

"I am grateful to have you with me," says Notah. "I am still very curious though, what are the weapons you carry? Why do you wear such ornate armor? What do the symbols on the poles your warriors wear on their backs mean?"

"Hrmm," grumbles Takeda, "so inquisitive. I will tell you more, but you must have patience young Notah-kun. Let us enjoy this conversation."

"Yes, *sensei*," replies Notah.

"The long spears we carry are called *Jumonji yari*, and the swords, long knives as you see them, are our *uchigatana*. Their blades glow white, with blue steel edges because they are blessed with light from the *tree of life*. They can cut through any darkness or evil. Although they look like staffs, because they are unstrung, some of my *ashigaru* carry a *yumi*, or longbow. At camp, they will sometimes train with a *bokken*, or wooden sword."

"Our armor," Takeda continues "is made in normal fashion of all Nihon warriors with one exception, we wear the colors of our cousin the Hotaru. The metal plates sown into our *haidate*, or thigh guards, also glow with the same light as our blades.

There are ten warriors with poles holding banners attached to the backs of their armor; these banners are called *sashimono*. The design is far more ornate that you would normally find in Nihon." Takeda leans in toward Notah's ear and whispers, "But we are not from Nihon." He sits back upright and continues, "*Sashimono* are worn by squad leaders. The squad leaders have five men each and follow the directions of their samurai. We are a small army of fifty-three warriors."

"The symbol is beautiful, Kenshin-san. What does it mean?" asks Notah.

"The *sashimono* is not only our clan symbol, but it also tells our story. The white banner represents the white of the *tree of life*; the light of *Tengoku*, or as you call it, the Spirit Lands. It is held to the pole by golden loops to signify our connection to our firefly cousins. A great mountain with a *torii*[23] on top to show we were once blessed and lived a higher

---

[23] Pronounced tohr-ee—"gate" (translated from Japanese).

calling. The lotus at the bottom of the mountain is our new home. It is all surrounded by the rising sun of Nihon." Takeda stands up on Notah's shoulder, still holding onto his bow for stability.

"We practice what is called *Bushido*, or the way of warrior," continues Takeda. "It is a code of honor and ideals that dictate our way of life. We are loyal to the creator and those placed over us by him until death. We train in the mastery of martial arts, weaponry, and warfare, but also in honor, duty, self-discipline, and self-sacrifice; tempered by wisdom, patience, and serenity. What *you* see, Notah-kun are warriors, but we are more than that." Takeda pauses, and then in a surprising soft, yet proud voice says, "We are also craftsmen, blacksmiths, farmers, artists, poets, monks, and teachers."

"Thank you, *sensei*." Notah, contemplating all that he has learned is finally quiet. Takeda bows slightly, and then stretches his translucent wings out. He slowly takes flight and goes to speak with his samurai. *Wind Walker was right*, thinks Notah, *my people and the Hotaru-Raikō share so many qualities*. He and Takeda enjoy more friendly discussion along the way, making the day's travel go by quickly. A deeper bond grows between them. His confidence also grows and he is more determined to complete the task for the Great Spirit, his tribe, and his new brother-friends.

*****

After crossing Aha Kwahwat, they follow it southwest for three days. Notah knows the river makes large, southward bends before coming back to the northwest. After three days, he turns away from the river, taking the high ground due west, which saves valuable time. He reaches the north side of the great canyon in one day. There are several springs there. The expedition replenishes their provisions and continues due west until they reach the place where the Aha Kwahwat flows south. Directly north of this southward turn is a place called Black Mesa. The Lowlands between feel like a natural gateway toward the desert.

Notah stops at the riverside to rest and refresh himself. There, he spots tracks that change from coyote to human and back to coyote. The tracks are old and faded, but they are easily recognizable. The find lifts his spirit. *Lost One stopped here too before moving on.* He thinks to himself. *The Paiute people told of a large, lush spring northwest of the river bend called Painted Ground[24]. We can travel there for rest and provisions before winding through Red Rocks Canyon and crossing the desert to the Black Mountains.*

✳✳✳✳✳

They travel around the southern side of the spring and made camp just west of it. Notah hunts for small game and fills his water skins at the spring, while the Hotaru-Raikō gather cactus flower and mesquite tree flowers. Later, Takeda, Sasaki, Hatano, and a few other *ashigaru* sit on rocks close to the campfire. They sip nectar and, like warriors often do, regale each other with stories from past adventures or battles. They still laugh about Hasegawa's battle with the netted rabbits too. Notah takes great pleasure in listening to all their tales; he learns much from them.

Everyone eats to a full belly and things begin to quiet down when Wrestles with Hare asks Notah for one of his people's stories. He happily obliges. "We will reach Tomesha in two moons," says Notah, "it is a desolate place now, but… it was not always so. I will tell you the story of how it came to be called *ground afire.*" Only the crackling of the fire is heard as Notah begins his tale.

---

[24] A.k.a. Tule Springs

"According to an ancient legend, Tomesha was not always the dry barren place it is now. The valley was once fertile and incredibly beautiful. Fresh water springs were many. A majestic lake surrounded by giant mesquite trees and lush vegetation filled the valley. My ancestors settled around spring pools and meadows on the high lands. They grew many crops of corn, beans, squash, and sunflowers. They harvested mesquite seed pods, gathered pine nuts, and roamed the surrounding mountains to hunt deer and antelope. Their connection to the land was strong.

"In those days, they were called the *Timbisha* and were ruled by a beautiful queen. But she was vain, demanding, and desired a palace of her own—one greater than anything her neighbors to the South had ever built. She ordered her people to build this palace. She forced them to transport magnificent stones and timber to the building site to construct it.

"In the beginning, the Timbisha worked hard to please their queen. They dragged and hauled stone and log over long distances. Considering it their duty, they did not complain because royalty was sacred. However, as the years passed, the queen feared she would die before the palace was completed. She became more and more demanding, even insisting her own family work alongside the rest of her tribe. Gradually, they became a tribe of slaves. The queen lashed their naked backs if they slowed during the noonday heat. She even flogged her own daughter when she thought the girl was working too slowly.

"The princess dropped her load of stone upon being struck and turned on her mother, cursing her and the kingdom she sought to build. The princess then sank to the ground, overcome by heat and exhaustion, and died. Only then did the Queen realize how greed and obsession had corrupted her. She became painfully aware of how she had enslaved her own people, subjugating a tribe rich in family values with a love of nature. Her remorse and insight came too late though. The land itself also turned on her, punishing her for her wickedness and shortsightedness. The sun grew hotter and brighter causing the plant life to wither, the lake to dry up, and the animals to flee.

"The once fertile valley was soon a scorched desert. Many Timbisha fled or died of starvation. Eventually, only the queen and her half-finished palace remained. She was struck ill with fever. With no one to soothe or care for her, she died alone in the parched valley. Her empty palace crumbled, its stone and timber reclaimed by Mother Nature. It is said that spirits of the old warriors still haunt the land protecting weary travelers from the evil she allowed to consume the land."

All is quiet. The *ashigaru* contemplate the story. Takeda gives Notah a slight bow in gratitude for it. Notah returns the bow before warming himself by the small fire in the chilly night air for a short time. He then returns to weaving his lightning seed basket. He looks up at the moon; it is a little more than half full now. They are running out of time.

*****

Shadows dance on the valley floor as the sun turns the western sky gold, orange, and purple. The red and tan striped rocks change hues in the fading sunlight. They have reached the other side of Red Rocks Canyon. The ground is leveling out but it is also heating up. Notah thinks it better to rest now, sleep, and then wake up early to cross the desert under a darker cooler sky. The white moon, which is a little more than half-full rises between two peaks on the eastern mountains in the blue-gray evening sky.

He finds an old twisting pinyon pine tree to make camp nearby. He places his blanket there and leans his quiver, bow, and mostly finished basket against the trunk of the tree. Notah makes a small fire and draws close while the rest look for good spots to rest. Though it is hot now, nights can be chilly under the dark wilderness sky. He moves back toward the tree allowing for others to close in on the fire. Leaning against its sturdy trunk, he stares at the starlit sky. It has been a little more than two weeks since they departed.

Notah makes himself busy crafting a round lid for his slightly elongated, almost cylindrical basket. He has lined the inside of it with the rabbit pelts he cleaned. They would not only keep any seeds from falling out, but also keep the glow of their light from showing when he travelled. Now he constructs the round lid for the basket. On it, he weaves a decorative medicine wheel using different parts of agave and other plants. Takeda approaches slowly on foot and takes a seat near him, watching him work. "What is that design you weave into the lid Notah-kun," he asks.

"It is called a *medicine wheel*." He continues to work as he speaks, "The sacred mysteries are contained within it and it represents the outer boundary of the Earth. It represents the continuous pattern of life and death, the path of the sun and moon, and the shape of other parts of our culture. The horizontal and vertical lines represent the sun's path and man's path. Where they cross is the center of the Earth. Man is at the center of it all. We strive to find balance and a connection between our four sides, physical, emotional, mental, and spiritual. We also strive for a connection between what was, what is, and what will be. The East or red side represents the beginning, the ending, and the renewal. It represents the sunrise, the blossoming of spring, a light in the darkness—maybe the blossoming of a lotus flower?" He smiles at Takeda.

"It is typically associated with the spirit world of light, of returning back to our origin. The South, or yellow side, represents the peak of the sun's journey through the sky. The South receives the most light. It is responsible for the growth and flowerings of all living beings. It also symbolizes our inner child, our core wounds, and the rediscovery of wonder." Notah pauses to slide a strip of agave into place. "The West or black side is a place of sunset, the return of light to the dark. It is the autumn of our time, the end of our growing. The West symbolizes a place of transition, the shadow within us that requires introspection and confrontation." Notah stops for a moment and reflects outwardly.

"I believe this is why the Lost One took the lightning seeds west to hide them in the deepest part of the land in the darkest place. This is also why we must return them to the East." He continues weaving, contemplating, and speaking softly to Takeda.

"The North or white side represents a cold place of night, the winter of our growth. One must be strong in logic and beliefs if he is to survive his 'internal' north." Notah stops weaving and stares down at the cross in the middle of his lid. Something catches and keeps his attention fixed upon it. He does not think about the four directions, the four colors, or the spirit animals. Instead his thoughts and eye remain on the cross that lay at the center of the wheel.

"There," he mutters, "in the cross, lies the purpose of the Great Mystery."

A lone cloud passes in front of the moon, its shadow covers Notah. A shiver runs down his spine and an unexpected sense of doubt and fear cloud his mind. He looks solemnly at Takeda and says, "I am not sure if I can do this. I have made the journey but can I complete this great task? What if I fail? My father? My tribe? Will I survive or will I die?"

Takeda sees the sudden fear in his eyes. "Death in this world is not to be feared, Notah-kun." Takeda reassures him.

"The Hotaru-Raikō know, without doubt, Kami will not condemn us to oblivion. We trust him and serve him with the knowledge that, when our time here is done, he will bring us to Tengoku. He will bless us with peace and joy. He will grant us an eternal, and peaceful existence in the fields around the *tree of life*. Have no fear, Notah-kun. You are strong. You see the sanctity in all that surrounds you. I do not think it is time for you to meet Kami yet." Takeda stands, opens his wings, and then flies slowly up in front of Notah. He reassures him saying, "Besides, I promised we would bring you the rest of the way." He then gives him a nod and a smile.

The cloud moves away from the moon and a pure beam of moonlight falls upon them. Notah feels a warm sensation fill his heart; his spirit is heightened. He smiles at Takeda. "Thank you, *sensei*."

A sense of confidence fills him. He suddenly sees the world in greater detail; crisper and clearer. The light emanating from his friends seems brighter. The sudden change in emotion and senses makes him wonder to himself, *This feeling, is this the helper Wind Walker promised?* Takeda bows slightly to Notah, and then motions for him to join them at the fire.

They rejoin Sasaki, Hatano, and the rest of the *ashigaru*. Takeda says, in a more serious tone, "Notah-kun, if we are to be victorious, we must know our enemy. Tell us all you know about this skinwalker, this Lost One, who guards the entrance to Shin-au-av."

Notah's expression turns sad. "We are only to whisper these things. We are normally not allowed to share stories such as these outside of our tribe. However, since it is the Lost One, we all go to face, the story must be told." He takes a heavy, deep breath. "Long before I was born…" He pauses, "Lost One was once a member of our tribe. Legends say he was a skilled healer too. Unfortunately, he became consumed by jealousy and corrupted by an unhealthy desire for power; a desire to control nature, not to harmonize with her. He wanted to control his people too. Lost One's brother was a great leader of our people. Not only was his brother brave, noble, and wise, he was a good father and husband. He rose like the sun in the elder's eyes and they planned to choose him as their new chief. Lost One learned of their plans, his heart darkened even more, and he sought out unnatural magic. He was caught haunting our ancestral burial grounds, looking for ingredients to make corpse powder to use on his brother. He was cast out of the tribe by the elders, while his brother was elevated to Chief. In his bitter wanderings, Lost One learned of a secret society, a group witches who served the evil spirit. They had the ability to shape-shift into many animals; he coveted this power."

Notah is clearly saddened, even ashamed, to tell this tale. "Unfortunately, the power of the skinwalker comes at a heavy price—the blood of a family member. He was readily prepared to betray his brother too. On the night of a full moon, he slipped quietly into his brother's dwelling. There he silently slaughtered his brother's entire family. The Lost One collected two water skins of blood from them all. He escaped without notice and took the blood with three skins, coyote, cougar, and bear back to the witch's cave to complete the ritual in secret.

He acquired the supernatural power he sought and now serves only himself and the evil spirit. When in human form, Lost One clothes himself with bear skin leggings, cougar skin breechcloth and belt, and coyote skin hood. He transforms into the animal he wants based on the task at hand. Needing stealth and speed, he came in the form of coyote to steal the lightning seeds.

There is only way to tell him apart from other animals—his eyes. In animal form, Lost One's eyes appear human, and when light is shined on him, they do not glow, instead they will turn bright red like a man's. When he is in human form, his eyes will look like animal eyes.

It is said that Lost One, and all skinwalkers are hard to kill. No brave has ever fought him and lived to tell the tale. We would need the assistance of powerful medicine to turn the skinwalker's evil back upon him." Notah exhales. "Sadly, we are without such power, and I think trickery is our only way."

"Iie[25] Notah-kun, we are not without power," rebukes Takeda. "We have Kami with us always. We have but to ask him, and he will help us. However, in this instance, I agree with you, some trickery and distraction are in order." They spent the next hour formulating a plan, until Notah reminded them of the pre-dawn departure. After that, they all got some rest under the chilly starlit sky.

*****

It always grows colder right before the dawn; that night was no exception. Notah woke up cold, his blanket had slipped down around his waist. He was not drowsy though; his mind was sharp. The moon had set, and the stars still illuminated the sky, but a predawn glow highlighted the eastern ridge. It was time to go. He roused Sasaki and Hatano, who went on to wake the *daimyō* and the rest of the *ashigaru*. The group broke camp hastily and headed west in the cold air. The terrain was mostly flat here and, as long as the sun rose at their backs, it would be easy to follow the retreating night into the western horizon.

---

[25] Pronounced ee-yay—"No" (translated from Japanese).

The time before dawn, when nature awakens, is a spiritual time. The cool air, the vast open sky, brother coyote howling and yipping; it keeps their minds alert as they travel the dusty sage-covered lands. Near black silhouettes of Yucca trees[26] stand tall against the fleeting dark-blue sky. They look like giants plucking stars from the heavens.

Beams of blazing golden-orange sunlight shine down on the valley floor as it crests the mountains behind them. Notah stops, turns to face the light, raises his arms out to his sides, and greets Father Sun. He welcomes the warmth and light. Even the smallest ritual and prayer bring a balance back to his spirit, which in turn, gives him confidence to continue. The rituals remind him of his people, and he finds comfort in that.

As soon as they have better visibility, Notah set off on a slow run to make up time. They cross the first half of the desert before the heat built up. Once it starts getting hot though, they slow their pace to conserve energy. Stopping briefly for rest and shade as they pass north of Shadow Mountain, some of the *ashigaru* stumbled upon dusty tracks from Lost One. Brother Eagle also appears overhead, confirming they were on the right track. The land levels out, and they quicken their pace after resting. Each one of them can sense the closeness of their goal; no one wants to stop. Before long, the Black Mountains appear on the horizon, just as the sun sinks low in the sky.

They make a final push to reach the Old Queen's Pass before sunset. Notah stays well back from the ridge upon arrival though, so as not to be seen in the fading light. The setting sun would cast a bright yellow-orange light on the eastern ridge where they were, alerting anyone or anything in the valley below to their presence. He plans to come back the

---

[26] A.k.a. Joshua trees

next day when it is more advantageous. *Right now, it would be better to make camp, rest, and eat.* He thinks.

Notah leads them all back to the open plateau, away from the ridgeline. There, they built several small fires so there would be less light; and so any breeze would carry the smoke east, away from the valley. They all seem to take a collective relaxing breath. They made the long journey. Though exhilarated to finally reach Tomesha, they are all exhausted too. It is agreed that what they need is a good night's rest, some food, and time to prepare for the battle. They eat flowering cacti and roast cactus pads over their small fires. Notah, Takeda, Sasaki, and Hatano make plans to climb up the ravine to the peak right behind Old Queen's Pass on the next day.

3

IN THE VALLEY OF THE SHADOW OF DEATH

死

N otah stealthily climbs the ravine up to the cold naked peak behind the Old Queen's Pass. Takeda, Sasaki, and Hatano fly up one at a time so as not to attract any attention. Notah lay on his belly while the three Hotaru-Raikō, being only eight to ten inches tall, are easily concealed standing or kneeling next to rocks. In a moment of immature nervous levity, Notah nudges Sasaki saying, "It's easier for you to go unnoticed huh, little brother?" Takeda gives him a firm look and he knows to be more serious.

Down in the barren valley stands the shell of an ancient twisted old pine tree, just as Wind Walker said. No longer wood, it is a petrified black and rust brown color. Its misshapen branches look like flames frozen in time. At its base is an opening, a large black hole in the cracked scaly ground. Lost One, in his gangly human form, stalks the tree's fossilized remains.

Not only do Notah and the Hotaru-Raikō have the high ground, but they are also upwind, which conceals their observation and their approach. Besides his shape-shifting skill, the skinwalker's only other advantage is that he would be able to see them coming down the mountain pass. Notah suggests they wait until dusk to descend, just after the sun has set behind the mountains and the moon is rising in the sky. Takeda agrees. He will send his army north, fly down a wide gully they spot in the mountainside, and then approach him from there. Lost One should be distracted by their lights in the shadowy twilight. Notah would descend the ravine directly in front of them and south of the Old Queen's Pass. He should be well concealed in its shadow, as long as he stays low and quiet.

The Hotaru-Raikō will draw Lost One away from the tree so Notah can slip through the entrance to Shin-au-av. Takeda, Hasegawa, and one other will accompany Notah into the underground passages to help light the way. They can hide in Notah's basket during the approach so their light will not be seen by the skinwalker. Everyone agrees on the plan and they head back to the camp to wait for nightfall.

*****

Notah has never been in war. He sits on his blanket under a small pinyon pine in quiet contemplation while inspecting his bow. A warm breeze stirs the sand. He is acutely aware of the hush that has fallen over the camp. He looks around and sees the *ashigaru* sharpening their blades, adjusting their armor, or sitting in quiet themselves. Sasaki and Hatano move around the camp checking their warriors. The *daimyō*, kneeling on his feet with his palms on his upper legs, is in deep meditation. Notah fights an emotional upheaval, a nervous disquiet. He closes his eyes and breathes, trying to slow his rapid heartbeat and racing mind. He puts down his bow and empties his mind of everything except what he has learned from his tribesmen, his new brothers, the Hotaru-

Raikō, and Wind Walker. He thinks of the journey here and all the sights along the way. In his mind he seeks harmony with Mother Nature and the blessing of the Great Mystery.

Time passes. Notah has calmed his mind and spirit. He no longer fears, he accepts whatever fate the Great Spirit plans for him. With eyes still closed, he breathes in deeply and exhales slowly. Somewhere in the wide-open sky, a war eagle[27] screams. He opens his eyes to the faint moon riding just above the distant mountain range in the blue-gray heavens. It is time.

*****

Notah's party had already started down the ravine before the rest of the *ashigaru* made toward the northern gully. The army is much swifter and cannot begin their assault until the light has dimmed. Notah takes only the basket, his bow and quiver, and his knife with him. He has smeared soot from the fire on his face and hands to keep his skin from shining in the moonlight. At the bottom of the now dark ravine, he sets the basket on the ground and removes the lid. Takeda, Hasegawa, and the other warrior who flew down with him, now climb comfortably into it the basket while he holds it still. Wrestles with Hare lands in the basket and whispers, "Hrmph, trapped again with *usagi*.[28]" They all give a low chuckle.

"I will keep you safe, Wrestles with Hare," whispers Notah. "Are you ready little brothers?"

"Hai," whispers Takeda. Notah closes and secures the lid before gently swinging it up on his back. He secures the ropes over each shoulder and sneaks out onto the flat sun-baked mud. He walks as stealthily as possible, for as long as

---

[27] A.k.a. Golden Eagle

[28] Pronounced oo-sah-gee—"rabbit" (translated from Japanese).

possible along the base of the mountain. Many white lights are swarming down into the valley and he looks for the skin-walker's reaction.

Lost One has taken notice of the swarm and realizes they are a threat. He falls on all fours and takes the form of the cougar, which gives him exceptional night vision and quiet prowess. Notah sees him crouch and lay his ears back; he is preparing rush out to meet the charging army. He takes the bait and runs toward them, leaving the entrance exposed.

As soon as the Hotaru-Raikō are close enough, the *kyūdōka*[29] let lose a volley. Their white-tipped arrows look like tiny stars falling through the night sky. They strike their target like porcupine quills but the pain only angers Lost One. He jumps, and like a cat catching a bird in mid-flight, pulls one of the *ashigaru* from the sky with his paws. He lands on his feet with the warrior in his mouth. Although his claws have already done their work, he bites down to ensure the warrior's death before tossing him aside. They begin to circle around the skinwalker, striking with their yari and uchi-igatanas. He growls, then hisses when one of them cuts deep into his shoulder.

Notah seizes the opportunity and begins to run swiftly and quietly as fast as he can toward the old tree. His moc-casins are normally very quiet, but the parched salt-laden ground crunches underfoot. The basket sways from side to side with the rhythm of his run. The warriors within push their backs against the walls with their legs, so as not to be jostled around too much. He takes his focus off the tree for a few seconds to observe the battle. Notah wants to make sure he will be able to reach the tree.

Lost One stops his attack. He lifts his head and ears up. He has heard Notah. He wheels around quickly, and peering through the moonlight, sees him running toward the tree.

[29] Pronounced key-you-doh-kah—"Archers" (translated from Japanese).

The skinwalker realizes he has been tricked and he is furious. He lays his ears back while giving a loud growl. The skinwalker ignores the *ashigaru* and charges toward the tree instead. Running at full speed, his head does not move; his eyes are locked on the young brave.

"Oh no. He sees us," says Notah. "Hold on little brothers." He gives up trying to be silent and runs full bore toward the tree, his feet loudly crunching in the crusty ground. Primarily watching the tree, he glances to see the cougar's silhouette approaching rapidly. He's not sure if he can make it in time but runs with all his might anyway. *It's going to be very close.* He thinks.

Notah is only a few feet from the entrance, but Lost One has arrived. He leaps at Notah in full stride, his paws out and claws extended. Notah dives down face first into the course dirt. The cougar flies over the top of him, missing his target. He lands on his front paws first, which drag in the salty ground, causing his back end to whip around. Notah jumps back up to his feet. He is within reach of the entrance. The skinwalker lays his ears back and lets out a vicious growl. He has trapped Notah. Saliva drips from his teeth and tongue as he menacingly approaches his quarry. Notah, standing sideways and staring into the red eyes of the accursed cougar, inches backward toward the hole in the ground, feeling for its edge in the dirt with his right foot. His heart beats rapidly. He suppresses the fear rising in his stomach as he places his hand on the handle of his knife.

Suddenly, the Hotaru-Raikō swarm around both sides of the tree with loud battle cries. Their weapons glint in the moonlight as they drive toward Lost One, who stops in his tracks. Notah realizes this is his only chance, he turns, finds the opening in the ground, and jumps down into the entrance to Shin-au-av.

He lands on solid ground below and hurries down into the ancient underground passageways. He places his right hand on the tunnel wall, feeling his way down and out of Lost One's sight. He knows the *ashigaru* above will keep him from being followed, so although his heart still races, he goes a little slower. The rock wall feels strange on his fingers. The stone is both smooth and slightly rough; not jagged, but not polished either. Once he deems it safe enough to stop, Notah removes the basket, sets it down gently and removes the lid. "I am sorry for the rough ride, *Sensei*. We are in the tunnels now."

Takeda says nothing. He and the other two promptly collect themselves and fly up and out of the basket. Hasegawa's *sashimono* glows with a pure white light, illuminating their immediate surroundings like a torch. Takeda draws his sword. The light from it, and the other warrior's yari add to the light. While they climb out, Notah removes his bow and quickly strings it. He then places it on the ground, pulls out a lump of charcoal from the bottom of the basket, secures the lid, and swings it back over his shoulders. He picks up his bow, removes an arrow from his quiver, and nocks it on the string. Holding the bow and arrow together with his left hand, he offers Hasegawa the lump of charcoal with his right. "Here," he says, "we can mark the walls as we move down into the tunnels. The marks will help us find our way back out."

"Hai," replies Hasegawa. He takes it and makes a mark on the wall to the right of Notah.

Although Shin-au-av once belonged to an archaic race, it has since been overrun by monsters, demons, and corrupt souls. They haunt its once sacred passages guarding one of the last entry points to the underworld. It has also been said, however; there are still a few brave Timbishan spirits who keep the old queen and others from returning to the world.

It dawns on Notah that he doesn't even know how to find the lightning seeds.

Takeda, seeing the worry on his dirty face, reassures him, "Because our light comes from the *tree of light*, our blades should grow brighter as we near the seeds. We will light your way, Notah-kun."

Shrieks, weeping, grunts, growls, and many unknown sounds echo through the endless black passageways. Only the light from Takeda and his two *ashigaru* illuminate the soft tan stone around them. They pass connecting tunnels, which Notah is unable to see down. He cannot tell from which direction the disturbing sounds come from. He suppresses his fear and follows his brothers closely. A strange faint bluish glow unexpectedly radiates from a tunnel ahead. Weapons at the ready, the party approaches cautiously. They turn the corner and discover the spirit of a Timbishan brave standing resolutely as though he were expecting them. He cannot speak, but using hand signals Notah can recognize, offers to show them through the underground corridors.

The journey down the winding rock tunnels is a long and difficult one. No one knows how long they have been in the dark passageways. Hasegawa runs out of charcoal right before the narrow tunnel opens into a vast underground room. The Timbishan spirit nods at Notah, who thanks him using sign language. The blue-hued spirit then dissipates as though a wind scattered him.

They step into the room to find a narrow rock bridge arching over a bottomless black canyon. On the other side is an amphitheater shaped cavern. In the back of it is a stone altar, on top of which sits a black, bowl-shaped basket. A bright blue and white glow emanates from the top of it. Light from the Hotaru-Raikō weapons glows brighter, which means the basket must contain the lightning seeds. Coiled around the base of the unholy altar upon which the lightning seeds rest is the legendary and dreadful Unhcegila.[30]

Her massively long scaly body slithers slowly around the prize. Dark red spots all down her otherwise rust-colored back shimmer eerily in the luminescence of the lightning seeds. Two long ivory horns protrude in an upward curve from her skull just behind her eye sockets. A short row of smaller horns jut from the top of her viper-like head. Her black eyes seem sunken in their sockets while white pupils' glow from the center of them. Her long, forked tongue darts in and out of her mouth with a slight hiss as she smells the air. She knows the enemy has come. She raises her head and opens her gaping maw with a loud hiss upon being disturbed. A smoky, fog-like mass escapes the sides of her pitch-black mouth as two rows of needle-shaped fangs spring forward.

Notah stops at the edge of the chasm, which keeps him out of Unhcegila's striking range. He is not quite sure if he can actually kill the beast but he takes a deep breath and raises his bow. Takeda and his warriors fly swiftly across the canyon and to the right of the serpent, distracting it. There is no hesitation in her. She strikes with lightning speed, wholly devouring one of the warriors. Takeda and Hasegawa move to safety out over the chasm to regroup. Unhcegila begins moving her head back and forth spewing out more black mist. The cavern darkens, and the bridge is obscured from sight.

The black fog clouds Notah's vision. He loses confidence, lowering his bow. Unhcegila uncoils from the demonic altar and slithers toward the bridge under the cover of the mist. Takeda can see all this happening and yells to shoot her, but his voice is muffled in the black mist. "She is on the bridge! Shoot her now, Notah-kun!" screams Takeda. Notah cannot see her crossing the bridge. She is now within striking

[30] Horned serpent of Lakota legend.

distance. The snake raises her head slightly in the black mist and opens her mouth for the kill. Notah takes a deep breath and exhales. He remembers his uncle's hunting lessons; how the instincts of animals have a sinless purity about them. He knows to trust his own instincts. He calmly raises his bow, aims, and trusts his arrow will find its mark. Notah lets loose his shot. It whizzes through the obsidian mist, between her needle-like teeth, and strikes Unhcegila in the roof of her mouth with a loud *thunk*.

She violently twists and turns, slamming her heavy body on the stone bridge as she thrashes about. Turning back toward the seeds, she whips her enormous tail around and hits Notah in the chest, knocking him backward and off his feet. Unhcegila returns to the chasm edge on the other side of the bridge. Notah quickly jumps to his feet, draws another arrow, and aims blindly through the black mist. He still cannot see the serpent. Takeda and Hasegawa realize this. They fly down into the chasm, and then slice upward through the black fog; their blades dissipating the dark mist. Their approach causes Unhcegila to raise her head again. Notah now has a clear view of her across the bridge and through the fog. He does not hesitate; he lets loose the second arrow.

Now, what Notah does not know is that when Wounded Crow placed his spirit stick in his quiver, he also quietly blessed his arrows. The medicine arrow Notah had let fly penetrates the weak spot on her torso, behind which lies her heart. The powerful arrow finds its mark.

Unhcegila hisses and writhes in pain. Her serpentine body flops feverishly on the ground at the edge of the chasm. The great serpent is dying. She tries to raise her head for one last instinctive strike, instead her limp body slips from the edge pulling her down into the chasm.

Takeda turns and bows toward Notah. He and Hasegawa fly to either side of him to light his way as he cautiously traverses the arched bridge. He then humbly moves toward the altar. Grabbing the rudely crafted black basket, he slowly lifts and then lowers it to the ground. Notah sees the lightning seeds for the first time. They are not quite what he expects. They're large and kernel shaped-like maize, yet translucent. He is mesmerized by the tiny lightning sparking and arcing inside each of them; they seem to pulse with life. Takeda and Hasegawa come close, their armor and weapons glow brighter yet.

"Hurry, Notah-kun, pour them into your basket." Directs Takeda. Notah shakes himself from his awe, removes his basket from his back and sets it on the ground next to the black one. He removes the lid and places it next to the basket upside down to catch anything that might spill over. He then pours every seed into his fur-lined basket, making sure to collect every single one. "*Yoi*,[31]" praises Takeda. "Now cover them and let's get back to the surface."

Notah tightly secures the lid of his basket. The glow from the seeds is gone and the cave is dark once again. He swings the basket around his back and runs his arms through the straps securing it over his quiver. The seeds are surprisingly light. He collects his bow and stands. With disgust, he kicks the black basket into the chasm. Takeda and Hasegawa light his way back over the narrow bridge. He pulls another arrow from his quiver, nocks it, and starts toward the tunnels without looking back. They find the last marking on the wall and then follow them back the way they came.

*****

Nearly halfway out of Shin-au-av, a demon long forgotten startles them. The hideous Dzoavits[32] charges the

[31] Pronounced yoh-ee—"Good" (translated from Japanese).
[32] Demon ogre of Shoshone legend.

group from an adjoining tunnel with a gruff yell. Wearing only an old tattered and filthy breechcloth, he is nearly naked. Long, dirty, and thin hair has grown from his head to his ankles, covering his pale skin. Behind the unkempt hair, large, round, yellow eyes glow in the darkness. Sensing the creature is about to strike, Hasegawa zooms in front of Takeda to protect him. Dzoavits snatches him out of the air with his left hand. He tightens his grip, breaking off his *sashimono* and breaking Hasegawa's back, who screams in pain. His *sashimono* and yari fall to the ground. The ogre shoves Hasegawa into his gaping mouth full of rotten teeth. They hear his muffled screams and a horrid crunch as the demon ogre consumes him, armor and all.

The tunnels are darker and more shadowy, Notah does not see Dzoavits swipe at Takeda and him with his right hand. He grits his teeth and groans when the ogre slashes through his shirt and into his left shoulder with his sharp fingernails, leaving behind four claw-like marks. Notah spins to his left to face the monster, while instinctively unsheathing his knife with his right hand.

Takeda, who dodged the second swipe, swoops down to pick up Hasegawa's yari. He sheaths his sword and picks up the yari. With both hands on the pole, he zooms up into the air, screaming in a vengeful fury. His armor and the blade of the yari glow much brighter, temporarily blinding the ogre. He buries the spear in the yellow eye of Dzaovits, who screams in pain. Takeda is slightly wounded when the ogre blindly swats him away. Notah ducks his flailing arm and then thrusts the blade of his knife between the neck and the shoulder of the monster. Dzaovits turns to escape, stumbling over the rocky ground and screaming in agony. He blindly gropes at the knife handle as he stumbles into the black tunnel.

They both know it is a mortal blow; he will not return. Takeda flies down to pick up the now lightless *sashimono* of Wrestles with Hare. He removes the cloth from the pole, folds it and tucks it in his belt. He and Notah pause for a minute. They mourn silently for the briefest of seconds.

Stinging from their wounds, the two return to the entrance. The sounds of battle are loud and close. They cautiously sneak toward the exit, only to find the skinwalker standing just in front of the opening. He has returned to his tall gangly human form now and stands with his back to the tree. Although he does not see them, he is too close to the exit for them to escape. He has many cuts on his skin. *The battle to keep him there must have been intense.* Thinks Notah. Then from below, comes the shouting of evils spirits as they scurry and scuffle in the passageways. They are coming to the surface in search of the seeds. Notah knows he is stuck. He must decide which evil to face.

Suddenly, a pink and orange beam of light shines ever so briefly through the Old Queen's Pass and across the sky. It disappears as fast as it came. "Day is breaking, how long have we been down here?" Whispers Notah. Somewhere in the distant unseen sky, above all the chaos, is the cry of the war eagle. A peace comes over Notah. He takes a deep breath, leans back against the rock, and says quietly, "Brother Eagle, please tell the Great Spirit we are trapped. We have the seeds but cannot escape the tunnel. We need his help." A shorter, fainter screech is heard as if in answer to his prayer.

The sounds of demons and evil spirits draw closer. Takeda looks at Notah. Though he remains calm, there is still an uncertainty in the young man's eyes. Takeda, grunts, "hrmm." He nods at Notah, draws his sword, and turns to face whatever might be coming up the tunnels. Though it is hard to see much of what is happening above, Notah turns to watch for an opportunity to slip past the skinwalker. Dark storm clouds roll in obscuring the morning light. He can no longer make out what is happening.

A quick flash of yellow lightning streaks across the turbulent sky, silhouetting the skinwalker against it. The streak is not only followed by thunder, but a deafening screech too. One so loud that it causes Notah to fall back against the rock and cover his ears. Then a second massive thunderclap trembles the ground, shaking dirt loose from the edges of the opening. The boom vibrates and echoes down the tunnels. The battle sounds above stop, and all eyes turn toward the Black Mountains in silence. The skinwalker moves away from the opening, out toward the mountains. Notah and Takeda look at each other and then bolt as quietly as possible from the caverns. Notah lifts himself out and then passes to the left of Lost One before looking up toward the ridge. He is awestruck and slows to a walk. The great Thunderbird had perched on top of the mountain range itself.

Its massive talons move on the ridgeline and large rocks crumble downward. Random beams of brilliant yellow and orange light slip past rolling clouds shinning on its black and blue-hued, feathery body. The legendary bird holds its body up with noble pride, while its head looks downward to the basin with great interest. Wind Walker stands to the right of the great bird. Though his own stature is rather large, his appearance is like that of a field mouse next to a great war eagle. He can be seen pointing down toward them. The great bird again gives an earsplitting cry followed by a loud thunderclap, "Skreeee—ka-boom." The ground shakes with its cry.

Lost One falls to all fours, his body convulses and contorts as he changes into a large bear. He then roars out in defiance. The Thunderbird wastes no time. It ducks its head ever so slightly, stretches its blue-tipped wings outward behind, and then thrusts them downward, fully extended, lifting its massive black body off the ridge. Gale force wind whooshes down the slope, tumbling stone and bolder as if they were small pebbles. Notah, and all the remaining Hotaru-Raikō, fly quickly to shelter behind the petrified tree and prepare for the impact of the wind. It slams into the tree, breaking off some of the stone branches around them.

The Thunderbird swoops down the Black Mountain slope. Lightning streaks from the white stripes on its feathers, arcing between the rocky ground and the turbulent sky overhead. The storm follows it; a deluge of rain falls on the slope behind the bird.

Lost One stands on his hind legs. Now 10-feet tall, he spreads his massive paws outward preparing to fight. The great bird pulls up as it reaches the basin and arches its wings, slightly slowing its descent. Its talons, twice the size of the bear, swing out in front. It readies itself for the kill. The skinwalker stands no chance against such a colossal bird but is defiant none-the-less. The mighty Thunderbird easily locks its grip around the bear with just its left talon. The bear desperately claws and bites at the reptilian skin and black bone claws without effect. The great bird rises up through the clouds, back into the pre-dawn sky. Feeling the bear trying to break free, it reaches over and pierces the skinwalker with his right talon. The bear now crushed and speared, lets out a final, faint roar, and then goes limp.

Notah scrambles out from behind the tree. He sees the rain waters from the storm cascading down the mountainside and runs as fast as he can out onto the salt flats, followed by the Hotaru-Raikō. The flood waters pour into the entrance to Shin-au-av. Demons and evil spirits below scream as the water washes them back to the depths from which they crawled. Notah slows to a walk, and then stops once he knows he is safe from the raging waters. He watches in awe as the waters weaken the ground around the entrance causing the trunk of the petrified tree to collapse into the hole. Salt and sand settle over it; forever sealing off the ancient city.

Afterward, Notah looks around for Wind Walker, but he is gone. Instead, he sees the bodies of several Hotaru-Raikō, who had fallen in battle. Their broken bodies settled in the water around the collapsed entrance. He and the others find and collect each one. He unstrings his bow and slips it into its case. Then he stretches out his arms, saying, "Bring your brothers to me and I will carry them to high ground. We will bring them close to the sky again." Takeda, Sasaki, and Hatano lay six fallen *ashigaru* across his arms.

Notah carefully, and slowly, carries them back up Old Queen's Pass to the same peak they used to observe the valley before. There he solemnly buries his warrior brothers under stones. They place one of their *sashimono* poles there to mark their grave. Takeda names the peak *Senshi no Maisō-chi*.[33]

Needing a moment of reflection, Notah walks slowly down the summit. He drags his feet in the sandy plateau. Fatigue is setting in and not just physical exhaustion; his mind, body, and spirit are all weary. He has not slept, he faced and overcome his worst fears, and now he mourns the loss of many good warriors. He undoes the braids of his hair in mourning, while trying to process everything that has happened in his young mind as he walks. On the ground, close to where the Thunderbird had perched, he finds a large black feather with a blue tip and a white stripe along its vane. He picks it up and looks skyward. Brother eagle circles in the winds over the ridge. Notah wonders aloud, "Is this a blessing or a reminder, or both? He takes a deep breath, and then says, "Thank you, Great Spirit."

---

[33] Pronounced sin-shee-no my-ee-so-chee—"Warrior's Burial Ground" (translated from Japanese).
Known today as Coffin Peak.

Notah turns to see the rest of the Hotaru-Raikō coming down from the peak. They all head back to their desert camp to rest, eat, and mourn their losses. Notah joins them. At camp, he takes off his basket, leans against the pine tree, and rapidly falls asleep.

4

NEW LANDS AND THE FEAST OF MANHOOD

御馳走

Notah wakes a few hours later. The Hotaru-Raikō are stirring as well. The sun is low in the sky. The nearly full moon is already visible and he is eager to leave Tomesha. He speaks with Takeda, who agrees that evening will be a good time to cross the hot desert. They all prepare for a shorter journey back to Painted Ground. Notah returns to the Old Queen's Pass and fills his water skins from pools of rainwater left in the ravine from the early morning. He gathers all his things and then leads the party east towards the rising moon. *It's always easier travelling with the sun on your back*, he thinks.

* * * * *

They return to the site of their first camp at Painted Ground. Notah goes to the spring to fill his water skins. A west wind had been blowing all day, which has been helpful to have at their backs. He crouches beside the spring and, while his skins fill with water, notices the wind blow across the surface. The water ripples like goose bumps on skin, which move across the surface with the breeze. They glitter with the sun. He watches as the breeze comes toward him on the water, waiting anxiously for it to reach him and soothe his hot skin. Those few moments are cool and calming. The simple beauty of Mother Nature restores his mind and spirit.

He decides to stay at Painted Ground until he can discern where his tribe's new lands are. Notah asks the Great Spirit which direction he should travel. While he waits for a sign, the party hunts, forages, and refreshes themselves in the spring waters.

On the third night, Notah sleeps peacefully under the full moon. Powerful vivid dreams come to him. He dreams of flying on the brown feathered back of Brother Eagle. They glide effortlessly on the wind, traveling north up, and over the cliff at his old home in Mesa Verde. He raises his face to the blue sky before looking down to see the ground below rapidly moving underneath them. He looks ahead as they swoop through arches and around tall pillars of tan and red striped rock before rising up and over another plateau. He recognizes the land of the sacred arches. In the distance Notah sees fertile grounds by a flowing river winding through the great basin. A soft voice whispers to him, "Leave tomorrow for *Seeds-kee-dee-Agie*.[34]"

He takes one last look at lush grounds in a valley around a river bend before his dream ends. He wakes, sitting up and looking around. The moonlight illuminates the spring lands. He instinctively reaches for his basket, which is safe by his side. Brother Owl calls in the still night, "Whoo-whoo, whoo-whoo." Notah knows where he is to go now.

*****

---

[34] Prairie Hen River (translated from Shoshone—a.k.a. Green River).

It has been over two months since Notah left his home in Mesa Verde. It is a hot summer afternoon and he is standing on a plateau looking down into a lush valley. A river snakes through old rugged mountains past the fertile banks. There is a small village below; he knows these are his people. He has been guided to this place by an unknown sense of direction, a gift from the Sustainer. He is happy to see his people again but he hesitates to descend the side of the plateau.

The last time he was with his people, he was content chasing lizards and playing his boyhood games. This journey has changed him. He reflects on his actions and experiences; he has seen many indescribable things and lost friends along the way. He wants to return home but is not quite sure how to explain all that has happened. *Will my people believe my stories?* He thinks. He wonders if he will finally be called a man, a warrior among his people? He went out into the wilderness, contemplated and communed with the Great Spirit, invoked the blessing of the Great Mystery, and retrieved the sacred lightning seeds. He has done what a man should. He should be happy to be home—still, he lingers on the ridge.

He watches a man, tall and proud, walk up from the river toward the village. The man stops, raises his hand to cover his brow, and looks up to see Notah standing there.

*****

Chief Ouray walks up the bank toward the village. He stops. Something catches his eye on the ridge above. There is a man standing motionless there, staring down into the valley and right at him. He puts his hand over his brow to block the sun from his eyes so he can see better. "Could it be?" He mumbles. *It looks like him, but somehow different.* He thinks to himself. The man on the ridge turns and starts toward the newly forged path winding down the side of the plateau. He carries a large basket on his back and is followed by tiny flying warriors. Chief Ouray's heart swells instantly and he yells, "NOTAH!" The tribe is startled by his outburst. Notah's name echoes down the canyon walls and the whole tribe turns to see where their chief is going. Chief Ouray walks toward the hill and is joined by a joyful people in welcoming their young brave home.

* * * * *

Three days later, a celebratory feast of elk, deer, beans, squash, and pinyon nuts is prepared. The morning before the feast, Notah goes before his father, Wounded Crow, and the tribal elders. He goes alone, bringing only his basket containing the sacred lightning seeds. The elders are sitting in a semicircle around a new ornate blanket, their backs against the cliff. His father sits in the middle of them. Notah sets the basket on the blanket in front of the council, removes the lid, and then sits on a rock a short distance behind it. The white light from the seeds brightens the alcove.

There is silence at first, but he soon does his best to tell the story of his journey, what he learned from the Hotaru-Raikō, how they worked together to retrieve the seeds, how Lost One met his end, and about his dream—how the Great Spirit directed him to the tribe's new home. The council listens quietly and carefully to his tale. When it is done, they sit in contemplation for a short time.

Notah stares at the basket. His thoughts retreat inward. To him, the elders disappear behind the light. Instead, his thoughts dwell on the splendor of Mother Nature. He recalls all the stunning beauty of the painted desert, the fresh water of lush springs, the vastness of starlit skies, and Brother Eagle gliding boldly in the clear blue sky. In his mind, he sees the smiles and laughter of his brother-friends. He thinks of their courage and Takeda's leadership. He laments the death of Wrestles with Hare and the others. He remembers Wounded Crow's words to him when he left, "I suspect that when you return to us, you will have found your purpose and the answers to many questions." Indeed, he had. He knows his role within the tribe should be protector of both his people and the seeds. In this, he has faith the Sustainer will help him.

Chief Ouray sees the somber and distant look upon his son's face. He breaks the silence. "My son," he begins; while Notah rises to his feet, "you have journeyed far. You bravely faced many evils and many fears, fighting to recover what was lost. You have restored the honor of our tribe. I, Wounded Crow, and the rest of this council recognize you as a man this day." Chief Ouray stands. "You are to take my place as guardian of the lightning seeds." He walks toward Notah, and is followed by Wounded Crow, each carrying one pristine feather from a war eagle. Notah's spirit is lifted. He knows what comes next and instinctively removes his simple headband, handing it to his father. They each fix their feathers to it. Notah bows his head slightly and his father places the headband upon him before stepping back.

Wounded Crow steps forward and speaks, "The elders recognize you as a man now, a brave warrior. We give you the name *Hania*[35]." He produces the long, ceremonial pipe and lightly presses tobacco with the bark of the red willow into the stone pipe. He lights it, and then holds it high in gratitude toward the sun, low toward the earth, and then toward the lightning seeds. The aromatic incense swirls around them. Wounded Crow partakes, and then passes to Hania. The ceremonial pipe makes its way around to each of the elders, its wispy smoke filling the alcove.

---

[35] Pronounced hah-nee-ah—"Spirit Warrior."

There is silence as they all share a grateful moment. Chief Ouray breaks that silence when he announces, "We delayed this year's Bear Dance, Hania. But now our tribe is whole again. We have settled into these new lands for a time, our scouts have returned with food, and you have returned with the lightning seeds. There is no better time than now to begin the celebration." Ouray places his hand on his son's shoulder and says in a quieter voice to him, "I am proud of you, Son."

The council returns to the gathered tribe, ready for the feast. Hania is presented to the tribe by Chief Ouray. All give thanks for his return. Hania sits next to his brother-friends, the remaining Hotaru-Raikō. Over the next few days, a spirit of understanding descends upon them all, allowing each to know their different languages. There is dancing, feasting, games, storytelling, and blossoming courtships.

Near the end of the ten-day celebration, Hania senses it is time to say farewell to his new friends. He carries the spirit stick with him on that last day. Removing the small medicine wheel from it, he approaches Takeda, who is sitting on a tall stone. He presents the wheel to him. "*Sensei*, my friend, all throughout our journey together, I would look at this medicine wheel and reflect upon its meaning. I do not understand why, but my eye continues to focus on the cross in the middle. The cross has deeper meaning and I will discover the truth of it one day. However, I offer this medicine wheel to you as a token of my gratitude and to remember the brotherhood we share."

The *daimyō* graciously takes the medicine wheel and bows to Hania. He motions to his samurai, "Yoshimoto-san. Bring me Hasegawa's *sashimono*."

"Hai," answers Hatano. Both he and Sasaki rush out of the feast. They return promptly, carrying a small folded cloth. Hatano approaches Takeda, who stretches out his hands toward him and, with head bowed, he offers Hasegawa's (Wrestles with Hare) *sashimono* to his *daimyō*. Takeda gently takes it from him. Hatano and Sasaki stand behind their *daimyō* and look toward Hania. Takeda reverently unfolds the banner with their clan crest, holds it up to Hania, and bows. Hania takes it and bows back.

Takeda says, "This is our gift to you Hania-san. It has been a great honor to fight at your side."

The solemn moment is interrupted by a curious look on Hania's face. "Hania-san?" asks Hania inquisitively, "I thought my name would be Hania-kun?"

"You are a man now. A warrior. You have earned our respect and will be known to us as Hania-san." Takeda then smiles somewhat coyly. "I told you we would bring you the rest of the way."

Hania gives a hearty laugh. "Yes, you did my friend. Yes, you did." They all join the laughter for a moment. Looking at the *sashimono* and saddened by the loss of so many brave *ashigaru*, Hania's laughter subsides. With a slight tear in the corner of his eye, and with the utmost respect, he says, "*Dōmo arigatōgozaimashita*,[36] sensei." He offers a low bow which is returned by both Takeda, Hatano, and Sasaki. The bond they share as warriors, as brothers, will last forever; it can never be broken.

As they stand a look of utter shock comes over Takeda's face. He and his samurai hastily land on the ground and bow low. The celebration comes to an unexpected silence. Hania turns to see the towering presence of Wind Walker, suddenly standing close by. Before Hania can kneel, the angel announces, "Peace be upon you all." He motions to all the Hotaru-Raikō. "Rise, my friends. Rise." He places his large hand upon Hania's shoulder and smiles. "Well done, Young

---

[36] Pronounced do-mo ar-hee-got-toe-go-zeye-ee-mah-sh-tah—"Thank you very much" (translated from Japanese).

Brave! The Creator is pleased with you. You have restored his faith in your people. He will bless these and whatever lands your people travel."

Everyone remains quiet, listening to Wind Walker as he addresses the Hotaru-Raikō. "Kenshin-san, Hasegawa and the *ashigaru* who gave their last full measure in this quest have returned to Tengoku. They once again fly in peace in the fields near the *tree of life*." Takeda bows deeply and says, "*Arigatōgozaimashita Omo.*[37]"

Wind Walker motions for the rest of the *ashigaru* to gather. "*Kuru*[38]. *Kuru*." The angel continues once they have gathered around. "You have all done very well, my friends. Kami is also pleased with you. He happily releases you to return to the lush forests of Nihon. Iku, live your lives in peace there. Watch over your cousin, the firefly, until Kami's son comes for you." There is a sudden and loud buzz in the air as the small winged army cheerfully gathers their things and prepares to leave.

They all assemble with Hania one last time. They all give a final bow to him, before taking flight. Takeda turns, waves his hand, and shouts, "*Sayonara kyōdai!*[39]"

Not only is it the last time he hears or speaks their language, it will also be one of the saddest moments in Hania's life. It is a pain that only warriors who have journeyed together, fought and bled together, and have had to say farewell to one another can truly understand. He will miss them greatly over the coming seasons.

*****

---

[37] "Thank you, Lord." (translated from Japanese).

[38] Pronounced kuh-ru—"come." (translated from Japanese).

[39] Pronounced s-eye-ohn-ara key-oh-die—"farewell brother" (translated from Japanese).

Now, legend has it, that on warm summer evenings, the *wakai josei*[40] will gather with fans in hand to gaze out over lush, verdant landscapes, spangled by hundreds of brilliant golden lights. There the hotaru meet to dance and attract a lover. Sometimes, around the outer edges of the fields where they gather, incredibly rare and tiny flashes of white light, almost like short bursts of lightning can be seen. It is said these white lights emanate from tiny warriors who protect the hotaru from anyone or anything that would do them harm. The wakai josei share the legend of Hotaru-himé with each other while they hope for their own prince to *bring them fire*.

---

[40] Pronounced wahk-eye jo-say—"young women" (translated from Japanese).

CHAPTER
5
THE LEGACY

"Countless seasons have passed since then, Grandson. Our people have known peace these many years," says Chief Hania as he stands up. Elu can see that his grandfather is weak and stands to help him if necessary. Hania moves slowly around the fire and stops in front of him. He holds out his spirit stick. "This is yours now, Grandson." Elu lifts his hands, hesitates, and then accepts the gift. Chief Hania smiles before slowly returning to his seat on the other side of the fire. He speaks as he goes, "My time is at hand, Young Brave. I have already given my meager possessions to our tribesmen, keeping only the spirit stick apart, which is now yours."

He carefully sits on his blanket and crosses his legs. Elu sits as well, curiously examining his gift in the firelight. Chief Hania continues his instruction, "The markings you see (蛍雷光) carved into it are called *kanji*. They are symbols for the words, Hotaru-Raikō. Wrestles with Hare's *sashimono* is sewn around the stick above them. The giant feather is from the majestic *thunderbird*." He pauses. "You must remember this, Elu—you hold precious items in your hands, but it is not what you possess that makes you a man. Your actions are what make you a man. Give thanks for what you receive from Mother Nature, for her gifts, her bounty, is sacred. Take care of your tribe, harmonize with the land and work to see the *great mystery* in all things; these are the actions that will tell others whether you are a good man or not."

Chief Hania pauses for a moment, he grows visibly tired. "Never forget, the evil spirit still searches for the lightning seeds. You are their protector now; they are entrusted to you for safekeeping. Remember one day, you too must pass on our story to the next generation. Our people must know the great responsibility entrusted to us. They must remain vigilant too."

Elu places the spirit stick on his lap and looks at him. "I will, Grandfather."

"Lightning is a beautiful thing, Grandson. When we see it, we know the *tree of life* is still alive and growing. The Sustainer sends the spring and summer storms to water the tree. The rain, thunder, and lightning are his way of letting us know he has not forgotten us, and that he still loves us. One day, he will let us climb the *tree of life* like children among the cottonwoods. We will climb happily all the way up, into his spirit lands."

Chief Hania takes a deep breath, looks to the sky, and says softly, "I am tired. I have done my best—Brother Eagle, let he who brings the rains know I am ready for the spirit lands." He looks through the fire at Elu who watches him closely.

"I am proud of you, Grandson." Hania smiles at him one last time before slowly closing his eyes. His head dips downward. He gently slumps over, Chief Hania has breathed his last.

Elu jumps to his feet. Still clutching the spirit stick, he rushes to squat just in front of Chief Hania. He places his hand softly on his grandfather's shoulder and straightens him back up slightly. He can see that he is gone. Small tears come to his eyes. "Thank you, Grandfather." Elu moves his shoulder to his grandfather's and rests him against it with his head down. He places his arm around his back for a last lingering embrace.

Elu takes care to release his grandfather in a way that leaves him still sitting but with his head down. He slowly, remorsefully loosens the braids in his hair, letting it fall where it may. Still squatting, he turns to find and collect a small handful of warm ash with his free hand. He smears the dark soot across his forehead and down each cheek. The tiny tears are enough to make it look black on his young face. He lowers his head, allowing himself a moment of mourning.

Elu raises his eyes just in time to see lightning strike the ground several feet behind his grandfather. He witnesses the white-hot fire burn the rock for a split second before tucking his head down and tightly embracing his grandfather. The deafening thunderclap that ensues stirs the desert sand and shakes his whole body. Startled and a bit fearful, he keeps his calm. He looks up to see two sandaled feet standing on opposite sides of the scorched lightning-struck rock. Elu lifts his head a little more to see a mighty warrior tucking his wings behind him and walking toward him. The angel glows, his wings lighting the night sky behind and around him with a subtle white light. He can only assume this is Wind Walker, the creator's messenger.

Elu stands, unsure of how to behave in his presence. Wind Walker is at least three heads taller than him and formidable in his appearance. He approaches Elu steadily, saying in a soft tone, "Hau kolá."

Elu's heart is beating fast within his chest, he does not know whether to stand, kneel, or bow. He humbly returns his greeting. The angel stops at the edge of the ring of light cast by the fire. "I am Præsidiel," he says, "but your people know me as Wind Walker. I come with peace and good news, young Elu."

Elu decides to kneel on one knee, asking nervously, "How may I serve you, Wind Walker?"

"May I sit with you?"

Elu looks up in surprise. He stands and motions to a place for him at the fire between his grandfather and his seat. Wind Walker smiles and steps into the firelight. He gently and respectfully leans Chief Hania's body back on the rock behind him. He crosses the chief's arms upon his chest and covers his lower body with his blanket. He looks as if he is sleeping peacefully under the open sky by the fire. "He is a good man," says Wind Walker, moving to sit upon a large stone. He relaxes his wings, their tips almost touching the ground on either side of him. He motions for Elu to sit too.

Wind Walker smiles as Elu sits down on his blanket. "Your grandfather walks the spirit lands with much peace and joy now." He pauses. "I have been sent to tell you much more than that though. I was sent to instruct you as I did Chief Hania, so you too will be an honorable chief—a noble guardian of the lightning seeds."

EPILOGUE

ENTERING THE
SPIRIT LANDS

I recline against a smooth flat stone with my arms across my chest and my eyes closed. All sound has fallen away. Everything, even the cool evening wind is still. I take a deep breath and exhale, a sense of peace, of contentment, moves through me as I do. Then a hand gently touches my left shoulder. In the silence, a soft voice, "Hania, open your eyes."

I open them to a starlit sky like no other; so much more to behold in it than when I was a boy. I sit up. A brilliant full moon appearing closer than normal, illuminates my surroundings as though it were twilight, not night. None of the landmarks are recognizable. To my added wonder, Wind Walker is standing in front and to the left of me. His wings, his armor, his entire body shine with a light I am not used to seeing. He offers me his hand. I take it and rise to my feet. I feel younger, stronger. Wind Walker smiles and says, "Hello, my friend."

"Hello." I looked down at my clothes. I am wearing clean light tan pants made from animal skin, decorative short strips of leather run down the sides of each leg. I have on a new long sleeve cloth shirt, light blue in color; over which is my bone, breast plate, adorned with small feathers. I look around in curiosity, asking, "What is this place?"

"You are in a place between creation and the Spirit Lands. This is the time of your reckoning, my good friend, when you will understand the deeper truth of the Great Mystery. All that you have done will be revealed, nothing is hidden before the One, the Son of the Great Spirit, our Lord Jesus, the Christ."

A blinding light appears in front of me. Wind Walker immediately steps aside, takes a knee, and bows low. Suddenly overcome with a deep sense of humility, I too, am compelled to kneel.

A silhouette appears in the light. "Peace be upon you, Hania." Comes the soft but authoritative voice.

A man, taller than me and dressed in the whitest of garments, passes through the light into the moonlit world. He has long, wavy, brown hair that barely touches his shoulders, and a full thick beard. His copper eyes blaze like a war eagle who defends its nest. I feel somewhat ashamed to look at him but cannot shift my gaze away either. He approaches me slowly. As he does, he opens his palms toward me. Light beams through the holes in each of them and land warmly upon my face. Unexpected knowledge floods my mind; I see the passion of the Christ, and suddenly understand the cross inside the medicine wheel—the real symbolism of it. I am saddened by this knowledge. Shame of my own misdeeds cause me to remove the feathers from my hair and lay them on the ground at his feet.

"The Sacred Spirit was sent to you many seasons ago," says Jesus, crouching down in front of me to pick up the feathers. He looks me in the eye and says, "Ever since that day in Red Rocks Canyon, you have contemplated the cross, its true significance. That is why I gave you the knowledge of my crucifixion. Since that day, the spirit has strengthened you, guided you, and revealed certain truths to you, preparing you for this very moment. Although you continued to live harmoniously with the land, you elevated your spiritual life. You believed, though you did not fully understand. Though your people care not for possessions, you cared for the seeds given to you by my Father. Though you, yourself, did not truly know him. You sought the truth of the Great Mystery. You did not know it was me you sought though."

He smiled at me. In his eyes are the love of a father for a son. Jesus continues, "I *am* the fulfillment of the Great Mystery, Hania. I am the way, the truth, and the life. None enter the Spirit Lands except through me."

He pauses for a second before standing back up. "Because you lived as I wish all men would, not bound to possessions, reverent of the gift of nature, and seeking the divinity of my father in all things instead, I gladly offer entry to you. Will you accept my grace, my gift?"

Without hesitation I said, "Yes, Son of the Great Spirit, I will." An unbridled happiness and warmth enter my own spirit. Though I continue to kneel before him, I could not stop the smile which spread across my face.

"I am happy. Well done, my good and faithful servant. Now please, stand."

I stood. He motions for me to turn around. "You faced true evil to save what is sacred, what is my Father's. By overcoming your fear, trusting in the Sacred Spirit, and recovering the lightning seeds, you earned these feathers."

He gently weaves them back into my hair. He pats me on the shoulder when he is done, and I turn to face him again. He says, "Like your earthly father, I too am proud of you, Hania."

The light behind him becomes brighter again. The angel stands quietly as Jesus turns to walk toward the gateway of light. He motions for me to follow saying, "Come

now, I think there are others who long to see you again."
He passes through the light. Wind Walker smiles at me, and
then turns to follow him. I too walk briskly toward the oval-
shaped light, and then through.

I emerge into a vast sunlit land. All around is a nature
far more colorful and brighter than anything I have ever seen.
More magnificent than the desert in full spring bloom. More
beautiful than the full moon rising over the sandstone mountains. More splendid than proud brother elk standing on a
grassy hill.

I look down and realize I am standing on a wide stone
path like I've never seen. I follow it with my eyes, it leads to
a city on a hill in the distance. It is like Mesa Verde yet much
larger and more captivating. Jesus is on my right, and Wind
Walker on my left. I collect my senses and look to Jesus, who
says, "Do you see the great white tree on the hill there?"

He points to another lower hill to the right of the gleaming stone city, upon which grows a massive tree of white light.
Hundreds of tiny, golden lights flicker in the tall grass around
its trunk. A youthful exuberance wells up within me. "There
are your brothers, Hania. Takeda, Wrestles with Hare, and all
the rest," confirms Jesus with a smile.

"They have been awaiting your arrival with great antici-
pation." I look at him with much excitement yet cannot find
words to express my gratitude. He laughs, "Ha, ha, ha! Go.
Further up and further in with you. We will meet again in
the great city soon enough." I bow my head to Jesus and say,
"Thank you, Great Spirit."

*****

I walk with a purposeful stride and a deep joy up the
road toward the tree. I contemplate the Sacred Spirit (the sustainer); Jesus, son of the Creator; and the Great Spirit himself

on my journey. These three make up the Great Mystery that I now have all of eternity to ponder with awe and gratitude. I will be forever thankful for their love, their help, their mercy and forgiveness—their great gift. At this moment, however, I desperately wish to see my brother-friends again. How I missed them!

I leave the road when it turns to the left toward the great city. I step out into the grasslands with my hands out to my sides. The soothing grass feels good as it brushes my palms. I have never seen such tall, bright green grasslands. The sprawling field leading up the hill is covered in it. A light and fragrant breeze blows across its surface and the grass moves and sways, like waves on the water. I stop for a second just to feel the breeze move and watch the grass dance with it. I look up to the tree in utter amazement. Though it is made of lightning, it keeps its shape. Billowing, light gray clouds with white linings surround its silver-leafed canopy. Far behind it are enormous, snowcapped mountains. From my vantage point, the tree stands out even more against their dark rocky bases.

Tiny golden lights of the firefly intermingle and dance with brighter white lights around the trunk of the tree. The Hotaru-Raikō no longer wear armor or carry weapons; there is no need for them here. Instead they wear more formal *montsuki haori hakama*[41] as they celebrate everlasting peace. I linger in the tall grass watching them for a moment. Their perfectly choreographed dance is beautiful to observe.

Soon though, vigilant as ever, Takeda Kenshin spots me standing in the field below the tree. "Hania-san!" He shouts. The Hotaru-Raikō stop dancing. An unexpected group cheer goes up. Then, swift as ever, my little brothers are streaking down the lush hillside toward me, the buzzing of their wings and the white light from their clothes blazes bright just above

---

[41] Essentially, Japanese formal dress.

the swaying grass like shooting stars. A tremendous joy fills my heart and my eyes fill with tears of joy. Hasegawa is leading the charge. "Wrestles with Hare!" I exclaim before running up the hill with all the cheerfulness of a child. Finally, I go to meet my brothers under the *tree of life*.

The End

The truly brave man, we contend, yields neither to fear
nor anger, desire nor agony; he is at all times master
of himself; his courage rises to the heights of chivalry,
patriotism, and real heroism. "Let neither cold, hunger,
nor pain, nor the fear of them, neither the bristling teeth
of danger nor the very jaws of death itself, prevent you
from doing a good deed," said an old chief to a scout.

—Charles Alexander Eastman

ABOUT THE AUTHOR

John Eudy is a twenty-six-year military veteran. He was both a soldier in the Army National Guard and a sailor in the U.S. Coast Guard. He is well travelled. Not only has he lived in ten different towns and cities in five states but has also visited forty other states, including Guam. He retired from military service in 2015.

After spending three short years as a human resources professional, John officially retired to not only pursue personal interests, including his dream of becoming a published author, but also to become a stay-at-home dad for his two daughters.

John and his family currently reside in their native Missouri. He has been married to his lovely wife of over twenty-five years, and they are the proud parents of four children, two of which are already with God in heaven.

CPSIA information can be obtained
at www.ICGtesting.com
Printed in the USA
LVHW020400021121
702171LV00005B/97